RUGBY
RUNNER

GERARD SIGGINS was born in Dublin and has lived almost all his life in the shadow of Lansdowne Road; he's been attending rugby matches there since he was small enough for his dad to lift him over the turnstiles. He is a sports journalist and worked for the *Sunday Tribune* for many years. His other books about rugby player Eoin Madden, *Rugby Spirit*, *Rugby Warrior*, *Rugby Rebel* and *Rugby Flyer* are also published by The O'Brien Press.

RUGBY
RUNNER

GERARD SIGGINS

THE O'BRIEN PRESS
DUBLIN

First published 2017 by
The O'Brien Press Ltd,
12 Terenure Road East, Rathgar,
Dublin 6, Ireland
D06 HD27
Tel: +353 1 4923333; Fax: +353 1 4922777
E-mail: books@obrien.ie.
Website: www.obrien.ie

ISBN: 978-1-84717-913-5

8 7 6 5 4 3 2 1
20 19 18 17

Printed and bound by CPI Group (UK) Ltd, Croydon, CR0 4YY
The paper in this book is produced using pulp from managed forests.

Published in:

DUBLIN
UNESCO
City of Literature

DEDICATION

To the late Seán Young

ACKNOWLEDGEMENTS

Thanks, as always, to Martha, Jack, Lucy and Billy who give me room to write Eoin's adventures, and to Mum and Dad who have been encouraging me to read and write for all my days. Thanks too to everyone at The O'Brien Press, but especially editor *par excellence,* Helen Carr.

CHAPTER 1

Eoin hauled himself out of bed and checked the bruises on his legs. He was still hurting from the tough week he had just had, helping the Leinster team to win a European tournament in London.

It had been a great experience, though, meeting and playing rugby against boys from several countries, and getting a chance to test his developing skills – and play in another international stadium. He wondered what his pals Dylan and Rory had been up to since they got back, too, but he would see them soon enough.

He peeled back the corner of the curtain and watched as the rain bounced off the pathway outside. Today would be a day to pack the bags for his return to school – something he wasn't entirely thrilled about, but that was coming up fast.

'Eoin!' came the call from downstairs. 'I'm dropping over to Grandad in ten minutes – if you get dressed quickly you can come too,' said his dad.

Eoin always enjoyed visits to his grandad, whose

house was on the other side of Ormondstown, the small town in Tipperary where he lived with his mum and dad.

'I'll be right there,' he called.

Dressing quickly, he popped into the kitchen where his mother was putting the finishing touches to a huge breakfast.

'Oh… thanks Mam,' winced Eoin. 'That's lovely, but I have to cut back on the breakfasts. You know… Leinster diet plan.'

'Oh, sorry, I keep forgetting. Sure it'll be time enough to start that when you're back in school.'

Carefully selecting the smallest rasher, Eoin slapped it onto a slice of brown toast and folded it in half.

'Have to dash, Mam, sorry,' he grinned as he followed his father out the door.

In the car, his dad asked him about the eating programme he was following.

'Yeah, I have to cut down on certain fats and sugars,' Eoin told him. 'They want me to keep a diary of everything I eat and drink, and to measure how much exercise I do. It's all very scientific now.'

'I suppose that's the end of your trips to the chipper with Dylan, then?'

Eoin laughed. 'Definitely. I must drop in to see how

he's getting on after I visit Dixie.'

Dixie was Eoin's grandfather, a famous rugby player in his day who took great interest in the youngster's sporting activities.

'I see there's a piece in the *Ormondstown Oracle* about you,' Dixie smiled as they walked up the garden path towards him. 'They say you attempted the biggest goal ever at Twickenham by a youth player.'

Eoin grinned at the recent memory. 'Ah, well I got a lot of help from the wind. And sure I missed anyway!'

His giant kick in the closing stages of the final in London hit the crossbar, but another Leinster player had followed up and scored the winning try.

'They seem a bit sniffy that you weren't playing for Munster. I have a good mind to write them a letter explaining just why!' said Dixie.

Eoin was at school in Dublin, and it was there his skill was first noticed by the Leinster selectors. It had been hard at first to wear the blue shirt – especially against the red ones – but Eoin had got used to it and enjoyed help-ing win the trophy for his new province just as much as he would have with Munster.

'Ah, sure don't worry about writing that letter, Dixie,' laughed Eoin. 'I don't want to get any more slagging.'

The old man made them tea and they chatted about

what was happening to the glorious treasure Eoin had rediscovered on his trip to London. Eoin's ability to see ghosts had helped him to put together two parts of a priceless golden egg, which he had decided to donate to the National Museum. Dixie was curious about the episode, but although Eoin and he were great friends, the youngster felt unable to tell him the full story – especially the bit about the ghosts! They carried on with the rest of the news around the town, before Eoin noticed the rain had stopped and the sun was shining outside.

'That looks nice now,' he told his dad. 'I might dash over to see what Dylan's up to. The packing can wait.'

'OK, but be home for lunch. And you need to give your mum some idea of what you're allowed eat!'

Eoin nodded and took his leave, jogging down the path and along the road back into town towards Dylan's house. His friend's sister, Caoimhe, was outside chatting with her friends.

'He's down the club,' she called out. 'There's some match on against Youngstown.'

Eoin slapped himself on the side of the head. He had forgotten that his local GAA club, Ormondstown Gaels, were having an end-of-summer series of games for the schoolboys and schoolgirls against their local rivals. And he had been asked to play!

Caoimhe lent him her mobile so he could ask his mum to dig out his GAA gear. He then rang his dad to ask him to drop it down to the Gaels.

Eoin hared off down to the GAA club where old Barney, the groundsman, was leaning over the gate.

'Ah, there you are young Madden,' he grinned. 'Sure they wouldn't start without you.'

Eoin collected a Gaels shirt and waited for his dad to arrive with his boots and shorts.

'You had a very exciting summer, didn't you?' smiled Barney. 'Off playing at Wembley I believe?'

'Not quite, Barney,' laughed Eoin, 'It was Twicken-ham. Same city though.'

'Ah, go on,' laughed Barney. 'Here's your father and grandfather now.'

Eoin thanked his dad for saving his embarrassment at being late and maybe even being dropped. The coach was relieved to see him arrive though, and accepted his apology.

'We'll have you at centre-forward Eoin, I believe you're a dab hand at kicking the ball from distance!' he joked.

Dylan high-fived Eoin and gave him some gentle banter over being late. His friend was still sporting the black eye that was the legacy of the injury he had received playing with Munster in the same competition in London.

The game went well for Ormondstown, and they were ten points up with a few seconds left when the ball went to Dylan, who was playing alongside Eoin on the half-forward line.

Eoin had shaken off his marker, and called for the pass, but Dylan seemed to be in a world of his own. He beat one man, and then, to everyone's astonishment, he tucked the ball under his arm and ran straight for the goal. As he reached the goalmouth – the goalkeeper had stepped aside in the face of this approaching marauder – he dived full length towards the line with the ball held out in front of him.

'A try for the Gaels!' he roared, before charging off the pitch towards the dressing room. Eoin ran after him.

'Dyl,' he called as they reached the clubhouse. 'Are you all right?'

Dylan stopped and grinned at Eoin. 'I'm grand thanks, just having a little bit of crack. Do you think he'll give me a black card?'

Eoin laughed. 'You're some messer, I thought that bang on the head you got in Twickenham was affecting you again.'

CHAPTER 2

The ref was so perplexed that he announced that he had already blown for full time, and there was plenty of laughter as the teams met up for cans of fizzy orange and bags of crisps in the clubhouse. Eoin joined the queue for the treats but after he had collected them he remembered the list of do's and don'ts in the Leinster Junior Academy players' handbook. And how fizzy drinks came top of the 'don'ts' list.

He asked the barman for a pint of water and joined his friends outside.

'That was some move, Dylan,' laughed Dixie. 'You reminded me of the story of how rugby was invented. They were playing soccer at a school in England many years ago when some lad picked up the ball and ran with it into the goal.'

'Really? And what was the school called?' asked Eoin.

'Eh, Rugby School!' said his grandad. 'The town was called Rugby. That's where they got the name.'

'So if I've invented a new game they'll call it Ormondstown?' asked Dylan.

'I suppose so,' chuckled Dixie, 'but that didn't look like much of an invention to me.'

'I could work on it…' said Dylan, already thinking of some innovations that would make his new sport more exciting.

'Well, we better head back and start working on the bag-packing first,' said Eoin's dad. 'We'll pick you up around eleven if that's OK, Dylan?'

'Sound, Mr Madden,' said Dylan. 'I'll be ready.'

As they arrived home, Eoin realised that he had hardly eaten all day, and raced into the kitchen from where some enticing smells were coming.

'What's that, Mam?' he asked.

'Well, I was caught out by that breakfast going to waste, so I dug out the diet chapter in that Leinster guide. That won't be enough for a growing lad, but I found a recipe for chicken and broccoli that seems easy enough. I hope you like it.'

Eoin smiled, delighted that his mum was going to help him with the programme, but he then realised he wasn't that keen on broccoli. He held his nose as he forced it into his mouth. This Leinster squad thing was going to be tricky.

After lunch, he sorted out what he thought he would need for the term ahead. His mum had ironed all his shirts and organised his socks and packed the suitcase full of clothes and essentials for boarding school life.

Eoin picked a couple of books from his shelf that he thought would be good distractions from studying for the state exams. He knew he had a big year ahead but some light reading would take his mind off study and help him sleep. He also lifted down a history of rugby that his grandad had bought him in the shop at Twickenham. As he riffled through the book he came across photographs of his old friend Dave Gallaher, and his new one, Prince Obolensky. He smiled at the memories that flooded back before carefully putting the book back on the shelf.

Next morning, with the cases packed and his two sets of rugby gear stuffed into his Castlerock College and Leinster Junior Academy holdalls, Eoin and his father loaded up the car.

'Is Grandad coming for the ride?' asked Eoin.

'I don't think so, Eoin,' replied his dad. 'He hasn't been great lately and he told me he thought the trip might be too long.'

'I hope he'll be all right for whatever final I manage to reach this year?' Eoin laughed.

'Maybe the Junior Cup again?' asked his dad.

'I suppose so,' he replied. 'We'll be under pressure to defend it, for sure.'

Mr Madden drove them around to Dylan's house, where Dylan was waiting with his cases on the pavement outside. They loaded them into the car and said goodbye to his mum and sister.

'Remember what the doctor said, Dyl,' said his mother as they pulled away. 'No rugby for two months.'

'Really?' asked Eoin.

'Ah, that's only the doctor being over-careful. I'll be grand.'

'You need to be over-careful with a head injury, Dylan,' said Mr Madden. 'Have a chat with the school doctor and ask him to keep an eye on it.'

Dylan said he would, and the journey passed quickly as they relived their exciting summer playing at Twickenham and made plans for the year ahead.

'Were Leinster on to you?' asked Dylan. 'The Munster coach gave me a ring yesterday and wants me to keep in touch and tell him how I'm getting on.'

'Yeah, they gave me this diary to fill in everything I eat and how much running and walking I do,' replied Eoin. 'I have this gadget that counts every step I take.'

'I wonder will we get a few games over the winter, or

will we get another trip next summer?'

'Yeah, I hope we have another chance to whip you lot again. Wouldn't it be great to have an interpro tournament and we could catch up with the Ulster and Connacht lads too?'

CHAPTER 3

Eoin didn't have to wait long for his wish to come true. As he claimed his bed in the dorm along with Dylan, Alan and Rory, he spotted, lying on his pillow, an envelope with the blue crest of Leinster Rugby.

'*Dear Eoin,*' it began. '*Congratulations again on the great performance in London this summer, and the club is delighted to have a trophy to display so early in the season.*

'*The Irish Rugby Football Union was also very impressed and has decided to institute an interprovincial championship for your age group. This is to help in the selection of an Ireland squad to take part in the Under 16 World Cup to be held in Dublin over the Christmas holidays.*

'*Ireland has never had an Under 16 team so the best of your age group will be making history.*

'*We will be in touch very shortly with dates of training camps and match fixtures but in the meantime we hope you are keeping up your fitness and diet programs.*

'*Yours, Ted.*'

'Woo-hoo!' called out Eoin. 'Hey Dyl, there's going

to be interpros for U16s this year – and a World Cup too!'

'I hope it's not too soon for me,' replied Dylan. 'Or the Munster doctor won't let me play.'

'Well, take your rest from playing and spend it running and getting fit,' suggested Eoin.

'That's fantastic news,' said Alan. 'Now, how about you tell us all about what happened in London.'

'Where do I begin?' laughed Eoin. 'Let's have a bit of tea and then go down the fields.'

The four friends left their unpacking till later and went down to catch up on the summer's news from their classmates. A lot of them had heard or read about his heroics for Leinster and wanted to hear more, but Eoin just shrugged and waved them away.

The big news was that the school team had lost one of its best forwards, Charlie Johnston, who had emigrated to Australia with his family.

'Ah, no!' said Eoin when he was told. 'Charlie was a legend. We might get a few more sausages for breakfast though, so it's not all bad.'

'I thought you were off sausages?' laughed Dylan.

Eoin's face fell. 'Ah sugar, that's right. I'd better leave them for you Alan, so.'

The foursome wandered down to the rugby pitch

where Eoin and Dylan told the story of the summer tournament. Eoin didn't like blowing his own trumpet so he let Dylan describe the dramatic final in which Leinster overcame Ulster.

Alan was wide-eyed as Dylan explained Eoin's final kick, but Eoin noticed that Rory didn't look quite so thrilled. The Castlerock scrum-half had been at training camp with him, but hadn't been selected on the squad for the tournament in England.

'What do you think about that interpro, Rory?' asked Eoin, to bring him into the conversation, 'There must be a chance you'll get in if Andrew Jacks hasn't recovered from his broken arm?'

Rory shrugged. 'I suppose so. We'd need to get a few good wins for the school first though. There's a mini-league starting with the schools around here and we need another Number Eight fast.'

As they walked back through the crowds of students buzzing with anticipation for the new term, Eoin caught sight of a familiar face.

'That's Charlie Bermingham,' he said. 'He was Number Eight on the St Osgur's team we played in the final a couple of years back. He missed out on Leinster because he broke his leg. What's he doing in a Castlerock uniform?'

'Duh, some undercover work as an Osgur's rugby spy maybe?' laughed Alan. 'He's joined this year; I was just about to tell you.'

'Hey, Charlie,' Eoin called out, signalling the new boy to join them. 'Great to see you here, what's the story?'

'Ah, my folks wanted me to work a bit harder and I said I'd be better at a boarding school so they sent me here. The rugby is a big bonus too. Any chance I could get into your team?'

'You don't know how perfect your timing is Charlie – we won't even have to change the name on the locker!'

CHAPTER 4

Eoin's mum had been at him all summer to remember that the Junior Certificate exams were looming at the end of the school year, and that he had to improve his grades. He wasn't a bad student, but he knew deep down that he didn't spend enough time studying. He had promised her he would improve this term.

It wasn't going to be easy though, as his rugby commitments mounted. Mr McCaffrey and Mr Carey had taken him aside on the first morning of term to tell him they wanted him to be the captain of the Castlerock College team for the Junior Cup. It was a huge honour, but meant even more time spent at rugby.

He had worked out that to fit in all the training sessions, games and fitness work around his school work and sleep he would have to have a twenty-five-hour day. The only way around it was to get up half an hour earlier and get a five kilometre run done before breakfast.

Eoin enjoyed the peace, plugged into his music player as he jogged around the inside wall of the school. Living in a boarding school meant you got very little time on your own and Eoin found he was able to relax and concentrate on his thoughts while on a run.

He paused as he passed the Rock, the landmark beside the stream where he had encountered several of the characters who had ensured his first three years in Castlerock had been such an adventure; Eoin had a mysterious ability to see and talk to ghosts, which he had first discovered on a school visit to the Aviva Stadium. Though it had been a real surprise — a shock, really — when he met his first ghost, Eoin had got used to meeting spirits, both in Castlerock and in other places.

He hadn't time to check if one of his favourite spirits, Brian, was lurking in the bushes, but he hoped they would meet up soon so he could tell him all about his summer exploits, and the Russian ghost he had met up with.

On he jogged, checking his progress on the gadget strapped to his wrist until he had completed the five kilometres. He warmed down with a few stretches and was just finishing up when Mr Finn came striding across the field to meet him. Mr Finn was an old friend of his grandfather, now retired from teaching at Castlerock, but still around to help and advise the staff and pupils.

'Good morning, Eoin, you're up with the lark today,' he called.

'Good morning, Mr Finn, yes I'm trying to get a run in before breakfast every day. I can't seem to find the time to do all that I have to.'

'Yes, I hear you are Junior captain this year, and congratulations on your marvellous displays in London. Dixie filled me in on it all. He's very proud of you, you know.'

Eoin blushed, as he always did when someone praised him.

'I'm taking your year for history up to Christmas as poor Mr Coghlan hasn't been well. I hope you hand up some interesting essays!'

'I'll try,' said Eoin, 'but I can't promise anything. Give me a few interesting topics and I'll give you an interesting essay.'

Mr Finn smiled. 'Well, I'll do my best too. See you in the afternoon.'

Eoin raced back to the dorm to dress for classes.

Rory was still in bed, staring at the ceiling.

'You OK, Ror?' Eoin asked.

'Ah, just a bit fed up, to be honest,' Rory replied.

'Why?'

'It's that letter from Ted. If I had a chance of getting back into the Leinster panel I'd have got one too. They've already written me off.'

Eoin shook his head. 'You said it yourself, Ror, a few good wins and they'll *have* to take notice. You were one of the top six scrum-halves in Leinster just a few weeks ago, and one of them now has a broken arm. You're playing on a school team that's one of the favourites for the Junior Cup, so you'll get noticed. Now get up and let's get double French out of the way.'

CHAPTER 5

School went quickly, with lots of chat about the new rugby season from all the teachers. The final period of the day was History, with Mr Finn.

He explained why he was filling in, and that while he would keep them up to date with their curriculum, he would be concentrating on ensuring they all finished their Junior Cert history project before Christmas.

'This year you can take a much wider approach to the subject, and they suggest you can write about how people lived in the past – what they ate, how they played, the clothes they wore.'

Eoin's ears pricked up. He loved studying history, but as he was nervous about how he was going to fit the project work in, he was alert to anything that might save him time. He put up his hand.

'Does that mean we could write about rugby, sir?'

'Well… I suppose so. Perhaps about the origins of different sports, or how they evolved… I'll have a think about that. Have you anything in mind?'

'I heard a bit from my grandad about how rugby was

invented and thought that would make a good project,' Eoin replied. Then he smiled to himself, and thought 'Between Dixie, Brian and that book I could finish that long before the deadline. Full marks, Eoin.'

Mr Carey took the first training session after school and told the boys that although he would be in charge of the Junior Cup team, he would also be bringing in a team of assistants to help prepare them for the competition.

He told the rest of the squad that Eoin would be their captain, which was cheered almost unanimously. Only Richie Duffy, skulking at the back, kept his mouth shut.

Eoin introduced Charlie Bermingham to Mr Carey, who was delighted to hear that he might be a solution to the problem caused by Charlie Johnston's emigration. Sure enough, the new boy settled in very well and even scored the winning try in the close A's v B's match that rounded off the session.

'Wow, that was a tough game,' Charlie said to Eoin as they walked off. 'We wouldn't go in as hard in training at St Osgur's.'

'Yeah, well, it's the first session. The guys are mad keen to impress the coach. It won't always be like that.'

Eoin spotted that Dylan had been watching the session from the sideline and called over to him.

'What's up Dyl?'

'I decided to sit this one out, but I think I'll try some light training on Thursday. I don't have any headaches so I should be grand.'

Eoin's face darkened. 'Don't be stupid Dylan, the doctor said you need six weeks off – it's barely been three since you were injured.' Dylan stood up to Eoin. 'I'll be OK, don't you worry about it,' he snarled, before turning his back and stomping off towards the dorm.

'What's up with him?' asked Charlie.

'Ah, he'll be fine. He got a bang on the head and he's supposed to avoid contact sports for six weeks. He's not a great spectator though.'

'You're a bit of a star here, aren't you?' said Charlie.

'I suppose,' blushed Eoin. 'Rugby's a big deal at the school and I suppose I've done OK. Winning the cups was huge, but it can be a pain with all the first years pointing at you all the time.'

'That's not a big price to pay,' laughed Charlie. 'Maybe you could get the first years to do your homework for you, too.'

CHAPTER 6

Next morning, out on his morning jog, Eoin called in to see an old friend; Brian Hanrahan was a long-dead rugby player who had been a great help to Eoin in many ways since he met him in his first term at Castlerock.

Brian usually turned up at the Aviva Stadium, the rugby ground on Lansdowne Road where he had been killed playing a cup match almost a century before. But he often called out to visit Eoin at the school, and the Rock was the spot they would meet.

Eoin slipped into the bushes and sure enough there was his pal.

'Gosh, Eoin, you've grown six inches since I saw you last,' Brian laughed.

'I know; my mother keeps saying I've had a stretch. My feet are too long for the bed in the dorm.'

'That's no harm. You'll be able to look after yourself better against those Munster boyos. Now tell me about what you've been up to.'

Eoin filled Brian in on solving the mystery of the jewelled egg and what he and Dixie had decided to do with it, and the victory at Twickenham. He also explained the busy rugby schedule ahead of him.

'And because the Rugby World Cup is going to be held in Ireland in a couple of years, they've decided to hold a mini World Cup for Under 16s as a sort-of dry run for the organisers. There'll be teams from all over – Italy, New Zealand, Australia. It would be amazing to get on the Irish team,' said Eoin. 'I'd have a good shot at it I suppose.'

'Well going out for a run at the crack of dawn is showing very impressive commitment. I'd pick you like a shot!'

'Thanks, Brian, I wish you were on the selection panel. Any excitement around here?'

The Rock was a magical part of Castlerock, and several other ghosts had appeared there over the years.

'Well, there was a strange-looking chap here recently, he wasn't very talkative, but he said his name was Will. He was dressed like someone from two hundred years ago, with a wig and buckles on his shoes. He seemed a bit distressed, but he wouldn't tell me what was wrong.'

'That sounds weird, I hope he doesn't make a reappearance. We've enough to do. Which reminds me, this thing shows when I stop – and for how long,' he said, pointing to the fitness monitor on his wrist. 'The Leinster coach will be asking me to explain and I have no plan to get into that with him!'

Eoin waved farewell, finished off his run, and after a quick change dashed down to the dining hall for breakfast.

Dylan was waiting for him, and he was angry.

'Did you tell Carey about the injury?' he snarled.

'No, of course not,' Eoin replied.

'Well, no one else knew about it, so how did he know? He's told me I can't play in any of the mini-league games,' he went on. 'That means I've no chance of getting picked by Munster! Thanks a lot, pal,' sneered Dylan, before storming out.

Poor Eoin stood stunned, holding his tray, while half the school stared at him. Although he was the star of the school's rugby team, he hated the attention that went with it and to be stared at like this was very embarrassing.

'Are you OK, Eoin?' asked Charlie.

'Yeah, just a bit rattled – Dylan went off on a rant there. He thinks I told Carey about his concussion.'

Charlie went red, and dropped his fork.

'Oh no, I think I must have let that slip when Mr Carey had a chat with me last night. I didn't realise he wasn't supposed to know.'

Eoin sighed. 'Don't worry about it, Charlie, Dylan's always been a hot-head. He thinks he's going to miss out on playing for Munster over this, but it's probably best that the coach knows. I was thinking about telling him myself.'

Sure enough, Dylan wasn't picked on the school team for the first game of the season, and he was difficult to live with in the dorm. Eoin had little time to social-ise, anyway, but he hated the tense atmosphere when the two of them were together. Once, he had started to explain what had happened, but realised he didn't want to drop Charlie in it so he stopped.

The first game was against Dodder Woods College, whose team included Marcus McCord, an obnoxious bully with whom Eoin had had a run-in at Leinster camp. They exchanged nods before the game, but there was no warmth between them.

Castlerock were too strong for their opponents, and ran out 22-5 winners. As they walked off McCord sidled up to Eoin and muttered. 'Did you get a letter from Leinster? The other guys here did.'

'Yeah, there's an interpro coming up,' replied Eoin,

not keen to extend the conversation.

'Hmmm,' replied McCord. 'They must have lost my address. My godfather is the boss of the main Leinster sponsors so I'll ask him to give it to them.'

Eoin shrugged, disgusted that any player would do such a thing.

'See you there, then,' grinned McCord.

CHAPTER 7

Sure enough, Marcus McCord's name was there in the squad of 45 when Eoin opened his post a few days later. Because he was captain, Ted had sent him the full list, and a few observations on how he was thinking about selection. Their first two interprovincials would be held in Limerick over the following weekend, and the last one in Dublin a week later.

Rory was wrong – he *was* in the party – and JD Muldowney and Mikey O'Reilly had both won a call-up too. Eoin was delighted to see Charlie Bermingham had been selected as well, taking the other Charlie's place for the province as well as the school. The new boy had settled in quickly and had impressed his team-mates with his willingness to work hard and never shirk a tackle.

Once the word got around about the selections, Dylan was beside himself with anger. He phoned home twice a day to see if he had got a letter from Munster, but his mother wasn't able to give him good news. Alan tried to talk to him, but he was so annoyed he just blanked everyone.

'I don't understand what his problem is,' Alan complained to Eoin. 'He's got a serious injury and Mr Carey just wants to make sure he doesn't do himself more damage.'

'Ah, but you know Dyl,' sighed Eoin. 'He gets in a tizzy over silly stuff. He'll cop on eventually.'

But Dylan didn't cop on any time soon. Mid-term break arrived and he still hadn't made up with his friends; he'd simmered down a bit and wasn't shouting at Eoin anymore, but they still couldn't discuss rugby or teams without Dylan blowing up or storming off. Eoin was travelling to the interpros in Limerick on the Leinster bus so they didn't have to endure their usual habit of going home together.

It was great to meet up with most of the lads he had played with over the summer, and to relive the great memories they had made together. The coach, Ted, too, was in a good mood and keen to ensure they were successful in the new competition. He stood up at the front of the bus before they left the Leinster headquarters in Dublin.

'It's only a few weeks since you lifted that lovely trophy over in Twickenham. Now I want you to concentrate on making even more history. This is the first interpro series for your age and Leinster very much want you to win it. Victory and some good performances will also ensure that we get the majority of players on the Ireland team for the World Cup, so please understand what a wonderful opportunity you have this weekend.'

The boys listened carefully, and cheered when Ted finished. Everyone had heard about the forthcoming World Cup and realised how close they were to winning a green jersey. They had all been working hard since the summer and were very confident they could do it all again.

Charlie and Eoin sat with Killian Nicholson, a player from Charlie's old school, St Osgur's. He had been lucky to make the final squad for the London tournament, but had trained hard and when his chance came he took it spectacularly, and was one of the stars of the final win over Ulster.

'How are you enjoying Castlerock, Charlie?' grinned Killian. 'Cold porridge for breakfast?'

'Ah no, the grub's not bad at all,' Charlie laughed. 'I could do with seconds sometimes, but it's decent enough. It's weird not going home after school though. I was a bit homesick for a few days but they're mostly a nice bunch.'

Eoin laughed. 'Mostly? That's not great gratitude for being allowed to become a bit more civilised. The only reason he got porridge the first week was because he hadn't learned how to use a knife and fork!'

Killian laughed while Charlie shaped to throw Eoin a few jokey digs on the upper arm. 'I'd say your rugby's improved though?' Killian asked. 'I'd love to be able to go for a run when I wanted, and you guys train a lot more than we do at Osgur's. We have to get two buses to the pitches we play on.'

Eoin nodded. 'Yeah, that's one really good thing, I suppose. The teachers are all mad keen on rugby too, so we get a bit of leeway coming up to a big game. The school goes wild when we win anything, so there's lots of good support.'

The bus pulled into the University of Limerick and the squad collected their bags before they were shown into a big hall. The local organiser, Persse McGarrigle, explained the weekend's programme to them, which involved a game the next afternoon against Connacht, and a second, against Munster, on Sunday morning. It didn't leave time for anything else except rugby.

Afterwards, Ted called them together and explained his plan to play two different sets of players in these first two games. 'I don't like the set up for this competition,' he explained. 'I think it's too much to ask you to play big games back-to-back, so that's why we've brought a bigger squad here. I may use some people as replacements over both games, but no one will play more than eighty minutes. But no matter who plays, remember this – I want two wins before we head home for the decider next weekend.'

CHAPTER 8

The players shared double rooms, so Eoin and Rory took one together while Killian and Charlie caught up on the news from St Osgur's. Rory was nervous, and having been cut from the squad for the London trip he knew this would be his second – and only – chance of getting into the Leinster set-up. Eoin knew Ted had left Rory on the bench on the side to play against Connacht, so he tried to distract him from the game.

'Will I be in tomorrow or Sunday, do you think?' Rory asked, five times in the space of half an hour. 'Maybe I won't even be in the match-day squad at all.'

Eoin shrugged, unable to give away team secrets until Ted told him it was OK to do so.

They wandered down to the hall for a bite to eat, and met up with several of the boys Eoin had played with and against the previous summer.

'Madden!' came a roar from across the hall, and over strode the Ulster captain, Paddy O'Hare. 'I was hoping you'd have broken your toe with that huge kick, and we wouldn't see you this week!' he laughed.

'Not at all, sure these toes are made of iron,' Eoin chuckled back.

'What sort of team have you got down,' asked Paddy.

'We've a few changes from the summer – Charlie's emigrated to Australia for starters – but the guys who've come in are pretty good too. Is Sam around?'

'Aye, he's upstairs fast asleep. I don't know why he needs his bed so often. He's in it more than he's out of it.'

The boys chatted for a while, exchanging banter with other lads as they passed by. Their talk turned to the forthcoming Mini World Cup, and who might win a place in the Ireland team.

'You're a shoo-in, Eoin, for starters,' grinned Paddy.

'I don't know about that,' smiled Eoin. 'You're pretty useful, and I hear the Connacht lad is a good kicker.'

'Really?' frowned Paddy. 'I had my heart set on getting on the bench as your shadow. I know I've no chance of making the starting fifteen…'

'Who do you reckon for scrum-half?' asked Eoin. 'Don't tell Killian I said this, but I reckon Sam has a good shout to be the starter.'

'I agree, he's got very quick hands and he's as brave as the bravest brave in Braveland.'

Eoin smiled. They went right through the team

making their choices, and agreeing on a side that was probably a little heavy on Ulster and Leinster players, but undoubtedly a strong one.

'Good luck tomorrow,' Eoin yawned as he said goodnight. 'You've an early start, but we'll drop down to watch you when our training is over.'

Back in the room, Rory was fast asleep and Eoin spent a few minutes staring out the window and up at the stars. He was fascinated by the sheer size of the universe, which always made him feel very small.

He looked across at the rugby pitches, now lit by the full moon, and was startled to see a figure standing under the posts, who seemed to be staring straight into Eoin's eyes. He was wearing odd clothes, and something that looked like a cloak, but he didn't move a muscle. Eoin continued to watch him for five minutes, but the man never budged so he went to the bathroom to wash his teeth. On his return he checked the window again, but the strange figure had gone.

Eoin had seen several ghosts over his time at Castlerock, and had no fears about them. But something disturbed him about this one. It took Eoin a while to get to sleep after that, and he didn't sleep well.

Next morning, before the training session, Ted told the boys who would be playing in each of the weekend games and divided the forty-five-boy squad to reflect this. Eoin was in the Sunday group, but Ted also wanted him to sit on the bench for the first game, against Connacht, in case of emergencies.

The session wasn't the best Eoin had ever been involved in – in some ways it reminded him of his very first back in Castlerock – and Ted grew more and more exasperated with the Saturday team. He had stacked his Sunday side with most of his best players, reckoning they would be needed more against Munster.

But the team he had planned to field that afternoon against Connacht was a mess. All the new players in the squad were in the line-up and they had yet to settle into the system the coach wanted them to operate.

'Quicker to the ball, quicker!' he shouted as they again failed to get to the ruck in time to protect their own player. The understanding of line-out calls was all over the place, and there was also little of the smooth relationship between the No 9 and the No 10 that was the mark of any good team.

After training Ted called Eoin over to join the huddle where he was conferring with the other Leinster coaches.

'That was a complete shambles,' said Ted. 'Now, I don't want to risk making the weekend worse by weakening the Sunday team, but there's guys out there that should be at home working on basic skills.'

'So what do we do?' asked the attack coach. 'We've picked the best from what we have.'

'Well, for a start, I think that scrum-half is useless. We'll bring up Rory from the bench – he did well when he came on for the last twenty minutes.'

Eoin smiled to himself. He knew Rory had been disappointed at being left out and this would give him a great confidence boost.

'Eoin, I'm starting to think we'll have to bring you on for the last twenty today. I promise I'll take you off early tomorrow – we can't be flogging our best player too hard!'

The rest of the coaches laughed, and Eoin nodded his agreement.

'This Connacht side aren't bad, but even that team should be able to beat them,' Ted finished, but he didn't seem too convinced by his own words.

After lunch, Eoin, Charlie and Killian rambled over to watch Ulster play Munster. Eoin was born and bred in the southern province, and cheered them to the rafters in the big European games. Maybe it was because Dylan wasn't on the team, or because he'd firmly allied himself to Leinster, but he surprised himself at how disinterested he was in the result of this game.

'Come on, Paddy,' he called out as the Ulster out-half made a break early in the game.

'Is that a Tipperary accent shouting for Ulster?' came a voice from behind him.

'Dixie!' Eoin gasped as he turned around.

'It is indeed,' said his grandfather. 'And your dad's here too, he's just off parking the car.'

'What are you doing here? I never told Dad where we were playing, just that I'd be home tomorrow night.'

'Ah, sure isn't this competition all over the local papers down here. There was a big write-up in the *Ormonds-town Oracle* all about how there were three lads from the town involved – I was sorry to see Dylan wasn't picked.'

'He hasn't been right since he got that bang in England and they've told him to sit it out. I think he'll be back playing for the school when we get back from mid-term break.'

'Hi, son, what time is your game on?' asked Eoin's dad, who had arrived wearing one of his son's blue Leinster beanie hats.

'We kick off half-an-hour after this one finishes,' Eoin explained. 'And I hope none of the neighbours see you wearing that yoke.'

But Bob Savage, father of George and Roger, Eoin's

pals from Ormondstown who were on the pitch for Munster, had already spotted him and was wagging a finger from the other side of the pitch.

Munster were no match for Ulster, who had been together for several training sessions since term began and looked very slick. Eoin's pals, Paddy O'Hare and Sam Rainey, dovetailed nicely at half-back and were the source of many attacks. Each of them scored a try, and Paddy kicked three conversions and a penalty in an easy 34–5 win.

Roger Savage gave Eoin as wink as they wandered off at the end. 'You've a tough job there Madden, they'll give you lot a serious going-over next week.'

Eoin nodded. He agreed that the Ulstermen looked very impressive, and that they would be tough opponents in what everyone expected to be the tournament decider. But Eoin was far more worried about the game that was up next, and whether Leinster would get their act together.

CHAPTER 9

Eoin was right, of course. Before the game Ted gave the team a serious talking-to, but too many of the players just didn't seem to understand. They saw their opponents as the weakest of the provinces, barely worthy of being on the same pitch as them. Eoin noticed several of the players sniggering as Ted's voice rose. Marcus McCord, who was playing second row, flicked his index and middle fingers against his thumb several times to signal that he thought the coach was talking too much.

Eoin was seething at this disrespect to Ted by someone who had no right to be on the team – and at the stupidity involved. He had only been playing rugby for four years, but he knew that no opponent could be underestimated, especially by a side that had shown itself to be a disorganised rabble that very morning.

When Ted finished, the boys wandered out onto the pitch in dribs and drabs, looking nothing like a team. All the spirit and unity that had been shown in London was missing.

And that became more and more obvious as the first

half went on. The Connacht lads were strong and brave, and they had a nippy winger. And while their out-half, Joe Kelly, was hampered by receiving the ball too slowly from his No.9, he was an excellent kicker and his skill in finding touch put pressure on Leinster.

That pressure finally told when he darted a kick over the backs into the corner, weighted just perfectly for the winger to chase, pick up and score beside the flag. The small crowd erupted, with all the neutrals delighted to see the favourites falling behind.

The conversion, far out on the touchline, was one of the hardest place kicks of all and Eoin crossed his fingers as the out-half took aim. And when the ball split the uprights perfectly Eoin gulped. Another penalty before half-time put Connacht 10-0 up and Leinster looked shattered.

Ted was white-faced with shock when he began to speak to the side in the huddle, but his features turned red with anger as he saw the blank faces of some of the players.

'Do you listen to me at all?' he thundered. 'McCord, take that grin off your face or, so help me, you will never wear that shirt again.'

The players were shocked at Ted's reaction, and all stared at Marcus McCord.

'I think I will, Ted – while that name is printed across the middle,' he snipped back, pointing at the sponsor's name on his shirt.

Ted's face turned purple, but he just about held his tongue.

'OK, I want you to keep it tight for the next ten minutes,' he said. 'No mistakes. I'm going to make a few changes half way through and hopefully we have more bench strength than they have. We can still win this, so go out there and do your best to make sure we do.'

However, his call for 'no mistakes' was almost immediately forgotten as McCord dropped the ball from the kick off and Connacht piled through the defence. Their out-half, Joe Kelly, kicked to touch right in the corner. McCord caught the ball in the line-out, but as he fell he slipped and the ball squirted forward to the Connacht scrum-half. With the ref playing advantage the Leinster defence was at sea and when Kelly side-stepped his opposite number it was a straight run in under the posts.

Ted's complexion had gone through the spectrum in the last ten minutes but Eoin had never seen him as angry. The coach signalled to Eoin to come with him for a quiet chat behind the dug-out.

'This is awful, Eoin, it's embarrassing. If we lose today there's no chance of winning this competition. That out-

48

half is just creaming us. We've no leaders – Rory needs to be more vocal. I'm going to send you on immediately, you're our best hope of salvaging something.'

'OK, Ted,' Eoin nodded.

As the players returned to half-way to restart the game, Ted gestured to the referee that he was bringing on a replacement. Eoin felt sorry for the boy he was replacing in such a humiliating way – and also felt under great pressure to turn the game around.

Eoin had a quick chat with Rory, passing on some of Ted's suggestions, but mostly just trying to boost his shaken confidence.

'It's 17-0 Eoin, we've no chance,' the scrum-half groaned.

'We need to run it more,' Eoin replied. 'Our line-out is a mess and they are trying harder than us in the rucks. But I reckon we can find the gaps.'

Eoin kicked off, and was annoyed, but not surprised, that McCord again fumbled the ball as soon as he caught it. This time he'd dropped it backwards though, and Rory was quick to the scene and able to tidy up.

Eoin had passed on Ted's message that Rory needed to be more vocal, encouraging his forwards and letting the backs know his plans.

'Now drive,' Rory roared, passing the ball to one of

the props and sending him off on a thunderous run. 'Support,' he roared, driving the rest of the pack off in pursuit and ready to take his pass or protect him in the ruck.

Rory's new attitude paid off five minutes later. Leinster had been camped in the Connacht 22, but without being able to break through, when the scrum-half suddenly plucked the ball from the ruck and slipped around the side like a salmon sliding through rocks.

'Chaaaarge!' he roared, rattling the Connacht winger who, fatally, took half a step back. Rory ran straight for the corner and beat the diving tacklers to touch down beside the flag.

'Nice one, Ror,' grinned Eoin. 'We're on the way back.'

As he lined up the conversion, Eoin was suddenly conscious that Joe Kelly had slotted over a kick from the very same place, and he made sure he wouldn't lose out in comparison, although his kick slid over just inside the post.

Ted had been right about Connacht not having as strong a bench, and as their battling front row tired he was able to bring in fresh legs and Leinster began to compete more up front.

Connacht kicked a penalty goal, but their forwards

conceded some needless penalties, and Eoin kicked two of them over the bar to reduce the margin to 20-13. But try as they might that was it until the last minute of the game.

Leinster won a scrum in the corner 15 metres from the Connacht line, and Rory held back to check his options. Eoin pointed right but glanced left, their code to confuse opposing defences. Rory took off with the ball, charging to his left and as he was tackled offloaded to the nearest man following up. He dived and just managed to get the ball over the line before being buried by green shirts.

When the dust settled, the last man up with the ball in his hand was Marcus McCord, a sneering grin all over his face as he made a triumphant gesture towards the Leinster bench.

'Try and drop me now, Ted,' he laughed, as he tossed the ball to Eoin for the conversion.

Eoin was angered by this new show of disrespect, and refused to congratulate McCord. He was still distracted when he set the ball up on the tee to kick what would be the equalising conversion.

He stared at the posts and went through his pre-kick routine, but was distracted by a laugh behind him from McCord, still basking in the glory of scoring the try. It was just too much for Eoin, who let his emotions get in the way of the job he had to do, and sure enough his kick was weak and sliced wide.

He hung his head as he walked back to the middle, and mercifully there was barely enough time left to kick off before the referee blew the final whistle.

CHAPTER 10

The Connacht boys went wild as their blue-shirted opponents skulked off. Rory put his arm around Eoin, 'Hard luck,' he commiserated. 'They don't all come off.'

'No, I was stupid,' snapped Eoin. 'I let McCord get to me. And it's cost us the game, maybe the whole tournament.'

Ted walked up and put his hand on the young out-half's shoulder. 'Thanks Eoin, you made a huge difference and nearly saved the game.'

Eoin shrugged, unsure what to say. He didn't want to blame McCord, and anyway Ted had his own problems on that score.

Dixie and his dad consoled him too. Eoin wouldn't be travelling back to Dublin with the squad, instead he would be taking the chance of spending a day or two with his parents during the midterm, so they made arrangements to collect him the following day.

'We've a team meeting now,' Eoin explained, 'I'd better be getting back to the hall. I'm sorry I dragged you all the way out from home for that.'

'Ah go on,' laughed Dixie. 'I've seen a lot worse.'

Ted tried to be as positive as he could be at the team meeting. He didn't see any point singling out individual errors, but he explained what the team had done wrong and how they might have executed things better.

He told the players to have a warm-down and a shower, and be back at the hall in two hours. It turned out the IRFU tournament organisers had hired buses to bring all four teams into the city for a meal and on to a cinema.

In the restaurant, Eoin took a fair bit of banter – especially from the Ulster boys – but Paddy and Sam were more sympathetic.

'What do they expect? You're not a miracle worker,' insisted Sam.

'I know, and they'd have lost by fifty if they hadn't brought you on,' said Paddy.

The trio were munching on their chicken when they spotted that the Ireland Under 16 coach, a well-known former international who had played with Munster, had arrived. He called by each table to say hello, but stopped to chat to one boy for more than five minutes. Eoin and Paddy looked at each other, nervously, and gulped.

'I wonder what he's saying to that fella?' asked Sam.

'Who is it? … Oh, I see him now … it's that lad Joe Kelly.'

Eoin did his best to put the day's events behind him when he hit the pillow later that night, but he was still seething at the antics of McCord. The big second row had been waltzing around the restaurant as if he had scored the winning try, conveniently forgetting all the mistakes that had handed Connacht the points that actually did win the game.

It took him a while to sleep, and his night was punctuated by vivid dreams starring Marcus McCord as a Frankenstein monster with the Leinster sponsor's name tattooed on his forehead.

Eoin laughed at the memory when he woke up, and resolved that today would be a better day.

CHAPTER 11

It *was* a better day, too. Ted had been as good as his word and took Eoin off at half-time but the stronger Leinster selection proved far too good for Munster anyway and ran out 27-10 winners.

Eoin was secretly happy that the Savage brothers had played well, reckoning that the more good second rows there were, the less chance McCord had of winning Ireland selection. There was no way the big second row was even near that standard, but who knew what strings he could pull.

Eoin and a few of the other players stayed back after the game to watch Ulster play Connacht. It was a good game, with the northerners showing a wary respect to the team that caused a surprise the day before. But Connacht tired in the last fifteen minutes and Ulster won by eight points.

Ted had been tapping furiously at his tablet, making notes and drawing diagrams as the game developed.

'We're going to meet up at Belfield on Wednesday,' he told the players. 'I'll talk to you tonight on the bus about the details. We'll probably get a run out on Friday too. I have a few plans about how to beat these boys and I know we have the players to do it.'

'I'm not going home on the bus, Ted,' Eoin explained. 'We live about half an hour out the road so I'm going to have a couple of days at home. But I'll be there on Wednesday.'

Ted promised he'd get Leinster HQ to send Eoin an email and the group broke up. Eoin sauntered over to the carpark to wait for his dad's arrival. He texted Alan to tell him how the games had gone and to say he'd be back in Castlerock early from the mid-term break. He hoped Alan would take the hint and come back early himself.

'Gr8 about 2day but bummr bout Conokt' he wrote. 'Ill try 2 get bak 2 sch Weds 2. U workin on projct?'

'No. I'm still thinking of an idea,' Eoin replied. He had never got the hang of how to write text language.

Eoin's dad pulled up alongside in the car and he tossed his bags in the boot.

'We were a lot better today,' he told his dad, filling him in on the result and how the game had gone.

'So it all comes down to next Saturday then. Maybe

your mother would fancy a shopping trip up in Dublin and me and Dixie could take in the game…' he mused.

'Well, I hope you don't mind seeing us getting hammered again. Those Ulster lads are good and I'm not sure we can get our act together in time.'

Eoin was glad to be home. He didn't get back to Ormondstown nearly as often as he had in his early years at Castlerock, and it was nice to get away from smelly room-mates and a menu that never changed. His mum always cooked him his favourite meals when he was home – though he had to phone ahead to let her know what he wasn't allowed eat anymore.

'Sure what harm would a chip do you?' she said when he came in the door. 'You're wasting away up there in Castlerock.'

Eoin laughed and hugged his mother, who ushered him into the kitchen where a steaming plate of food sat waiting for him.

'I have it all there for you – broccoli, chicken, sweet potato,' she pointed out. 'And to be honest that sweet potato isn't bad at all.'

Mr Madden joined them, and they chatted over the meal about what everyone had been up to since they last met up.

'Your grandad will be over later,' said his mum. 'He's

been a bit poorly lately but has been talking of nothing but how he wants to talk rugby with you.'

Eoin smiled, and after helping wash-up he went upstairs.

CHAPTER 12

Eoin lay on his bed, staring at the ceiling and counting the spines of his books to keep his mind busy. He spotted the history book Grandad had bought him and took it down for a browse, marvelling at how funny the players looked in the early days of the sport, everyone wearing a moustache and whiskers and big, heavy boots.

'Dixie's here!' came the call from his mum, and Eoin hopped up and raced down the stairs.

'Hi, Grandad, did you hear we won today?'

'I did – and many congratulations,' smiled Dixie. 'I hope you played well?'

'I suppose so,' smiled Eoin, 'Ted was happy anyway.'

'Well as long as you're keeping your coach happy you'll be fine,' chuckled Dixie.

The old man sat down and they exchanged a few stories about rugby coaches, before Dixie remembered something and reached into his pocket.

'I came across the name of the fellow I was telling you about,' he said, handing Eoin a newspaper clipping.

'William Webb Ellis was his name, and they even named the Rugby World Cup trophy after him.'

Eoin looked puzzled. 'Why?'

'Why?' said Dixie. 'Because didn't he only invent the whole game – remember, I told you about him back at the Gaelic match.'

Eoin nodded. 'Oh yeah, it was at some school in England, wasn't it? Rugby school. That's easy to remember!'

He read the clipping, which came from the *Ormondstown Oracle*, and told about how William's father, James Ellis, was once stationed in the town as a soldier with the Third Dragoon Guards, along with his wife Ann Webb and their children.

'That was back in Napoleon's time,' said Dixie. 'A long, long time ago.'

'It says here that some people think William might have seen a Gaelic match here and invented rugby because of that.'

'I doubt that, to be honest' said Dixie, 'but who knows at this stage. We'll never know the truth of it. But it's interesting to know that an important man spent some time in our town as a small boy, isn't it?'

Eoin nodded, slowly, and sprang to his feet and scooted out the door. He dashed upstairs, grabbed the book he had been reading, and returned to the old man.

'Sorry about that, I remembered the book you gave me, and wanted to see was there anything about William in it.'

The pair turned the early pages, and found a drawing of how one artist imagined William had made sporting history. With his white shirt flapping and his tight trousers that stopped at the knee, William Webb Ellis cut an interesting figure as he raced along with the round ball under his arm.

'It says here that his father died in a battle in Spain when William was six,' Eoin read. 'And that William never realised he had invented the sport.'

Eoin looked at Dixie and smiled. 'Thanks a lot for bringing this, Grandad. You've just given me a fantastic idea for my Junior Cert history project!'

'And of course the book will give you a great starting point. We must investigate more about his time in Ormondstown too. But it was more than two hundred years ago so it's unlikely there is any surviving evidence around the town.'

Eoin was delighted with himself, as the project had been hanging over him and he had been starting to get nervous about it. When Dixie left and it was time for bed, Eoin brought the book upstairs and started to read it from the beginning. There wasn't much about William in it, but he found it interesting how the sport had evolved to something that resembled how he and his friends played it in the twenty-first century.

Switching off the light, he was asleep a lot quicker than he had been the night before.

CHAPTER 13

Eoin may have dozed off almost immediately, but his sleep was interrupted less than an hour later. He awoke to the sound of someone scurrying around his room, rummaging about on the shelves and in his chest of drawers.

'Mam?' he called. 'What are you looking for?'

But everything went quiet as soon as he spoke and no reply came to his question.

'Mam?' he called again, switching on the bedside light.

Standing in front of the bookcase, clutching the book Eoin had been reading earlier with Dixie, was a strange-looking figure wearing long socks, pants that came to his knee and a long black coat. Under the coat he wore a white shirt tied at the neck. He peered through the gloom at Eoin.

'I say, you. Do you own this book?'

Eoin nodded.

'I'm in it, did you know that?'

'Really?' replied Eoin. 'What's your name?' although he already had a fair idea of what it was.

'Will Ellis, young sir,' replied the figure, who Eoin now knew was another of the ghosts from rugby history who came to visit him.

'You're the lad who went to Rugby School and ran with the ball, aren't you?' asked Eoin.

'I am, young sir, and what a to-do that was,' Will replied. 'I got into HEAPS of trouble with the masters over that. We were playing a game called Bigside and the ball wasn't being moved very much so I picked it up and decided to pep things along. The other chaps were quite angry with me, but it all died down soon after. Years later I heard about the sport, as it was some chaps from Rugby School who wrote down the first laws, but I was amazed to discover long after I died that they gave *me* the credit for inventing rugby!'

'Yes,' said Eoin, 'And they even called the World Cup trophy after you.'

'Yes – do you know about that?' said William. 'In fact, that's why I'm here...'

At that moment, Eoin's door opened and the light seeped into the room. His father stood in the doorway.

'Are you all right, Eoin?' he asked. 'We heard you call-ing your mum and then you seemed to be talking in your sleep.'

Eoin nodded. 'I'm OK, Dad,' he replied. 'I just had a

bit of a nightmare, I think. Nothing too scary though,' he grinned. 'I'll be fine.'

His dad went back to his room, but Eoin's midnight visitor never reappeared. Eoin picked up the book from the table where William had left it, and ran his fingers across the cover.

He shook his head. 'Another ghost for my collection,' he smiled.

Eoin spent the next couple of days of the mid-term break fooling around at home, helping his dad fix a few things and visiting Dixie. The old man was very excited about Eoin's project.

'Now, I can't possibly do any work on this for you – that would be cheating which is a serious business in a state exam – but perhaps I can dig out some pointers for where you might do your research. I'll head down to the library in the morning – would you like to come?'

So next day, at ten o'clock, Eoin sauntered down to the library on Chambers Street. As he walked in, he spied his grandfather chatting with a familiar figure.

'Hello, Grandad. Hiya, Dylan,' he said, uncomfortably.

'Howya, Eoin,' came the equally uncomfortable reply.

'Well, isn't that a coincidence,' said Dixie. 'I asked

to meet you both here at ten o'clock. I must have got mixed up,' he added, winking. 'Now, I don't know why you two aren't talking, but it seems to me that nothing should come between friends. You need to have a chat about it – and as libraries aren't keen on that sort of thing – chatting – why don't you two head outside and I'll have a look through the books here. I'll meet you both outside in half an hour and we'll go down for a nice cup of hot chocolate in Daisy's Cafe. You can take a break from the Leinster diet for once!'

Eoin laughed as soon as they got outside, and after a couple of seconds of trying to keep his face straight, so did Dylan.

'The old codger planned it,' laughed Eoin. 'He set us up.'

Dylan nodded his agreement, and the pair thrashed out the problem between them. Eoin apologised that he had let Dylan's concussion slip to Charlie, and stressed that he hadn't meant it to get back to Mr Carey. He also told his friend that he had been thinking of telling Mr Carey himself, as Dylan needed to take his injury seriously. Dylan agreed, and said he was sorry for being so pig-headed.

By the time Dixie came out with his hands full of photocopied sheets, the pair were laughing and joking about what had happened at the interprovincials.

'I'm glad you've sorted that out,' smiled Dixie. 'Now, Dylan, how is that injury. Is your waiting period nearly up?'

'It ends today, Mr Madden,' replied Dylan. 'And I've just emailed the Munster coach to let him know in case he's planning to make any changes ahead of the final game at the weekend.'

CHAPTER 14

Eoin took the bus back to Dublin that evening, lugging his huge rugby bag and his suitcase of clothes that had been washed, ironed and neatly packed by his mum and dad that morning.

He had brought the rugby book with him, devouring it as the bus made its way through the countryside, villages and towns on the road to Dublin. He also read the photocopies that Dixie had made at the library, and learned more about William's father, who died a heroic death in Spain fighting with the armies of the Duke of Wellington – who was born in Dublin!

He decided that, when he wasn't training with Leinster, he'd spend the next few days in Castlerock working on the project.

There were a few boys staying in school over the mid-term break, but his dormitory was empty. Eoin enjoyed the peace – it was a novelty not to have to talk to anyone and just read or listen to music.

Next day he took the bus a couple of kilometres to where Leinster Rugby had their base. He was very early, so he watched the senior professionals train for a while, and was impressed at the unflinching way they went about their work. He knew he would have to toughen up more if he was to make a career in the sport.

Ted arrived, and beckoned Eoin to join him in his office.

'Did you see the trophy there in reception?' he asked. 'The bigwigs here were very happy with us winning that – they've given me a bigger budget to play with for the interpros – but they're already moaning about losing to Connacht.'

Eoin grimaced. 'They didn't notice we hammered Munster did they?'

'No, they only notice the defeats,' laughed Ted. 'But another trophy would be hard for them to ignore.'

They chatted some more about Ted's plans for the weekend. He had been so impressed with how Rory had done that he had bumped him up the pecking order so he would be on the bench against Ulster. Eoin was great friends with Rory and Killian and didn't want to take sides, so he just decided to be happy for both of them.

Eoin asked Ted had he picked Marcus McCord, at which the coach threw his hands out wide.

'What can I do? The bigwigs are terrified of his godfather. He's not a bad player – although besides his try he was rubbish against Connacht – but we have four or five better second rows in the group. I'll just have to live with it.'

Out on the training pitch Ted took them through a few moves over the course of the morning, and at lunch told them he had selected two teams. He said that while the ones wearing blue were the front-runners in each position, he had an open mind and everyone had the opportunity to force their way in.

The coach stopped the practice game frequently to hammer home various messages, and Eoin was much happier with the way the team had started to come together.

Afterwards he dumped his kit in his locker and joined Rory, Killian and Charlie for a bite.

'No scrum-half talk, you two!' laughed Charlie. Rory grinned sheepishly at Killian.

'No worries, Ror,' smiled Killian. 'I'm a complete fraud at scrum-half – I never even played there till the summer. If you get on ahead of me, I'll be happy enough.'

'You've been working out since London, haven't you Ror,' said Eoin. 'You're definitely bigger than you were.'

'Well he's hardly shrunk,' said Charlie, 'He doesn't wash often enough for that!'

The boys finished their meal and sat through another Ted talk about the strengths and weaknesses of their Ulster opponents. The coach had a couple of ideas for moves and Eoin watched closely as he ran through the plays.

'Bo-ring,' muttered McCord at the back of the room, just loud enough to be heard by everyone except Ted. One or two boys sniggered, but most ignored it. Eoin shot him a look that signalled just how much he disliked him.

Eoin was still growling to himself about McCord as he caught the bus back to Castlerock. As he climbed down at the stop outside the school he was delighted to see that Alan was sitting there on the bench waiting for him.

'Hey Eoin, what kept you,' he laughed.

The pair walked back up the drive to the school chatting about rugby, and soccer, and school projects.

'I've decided I'm going to do it on the origins of rugby,' explained Eoin. 'I've got a really good book and Grandad found some stuff in the library too. It was a lad that used to live in Ormondstown that invented it.'

'Cool,' said Alan. 'I wish I had thought of something that interesting. My dad convinced me to do it on the German bombing of Dublin during the war, just because his grandfather was a fireman and worked there that night.'

'That could be cool too,' said Eoin. 'Did you talk to his grandfather?'

'Nah, he died long before I was born. They have a few family stories though, but I'm not sure that will be enough.'

CHAPTER 15

The boys were alone in the dormitory, but Alan busied himself on his laptop checking the sports scores.

'Do you know what you have to do to win the inter-pro?' he asked Eoin.

'Beat Ulster?' Eoin replied.

'Well, of course you have to do *that*, but you also have to beat them by at least eleven points. Look at this,' he said, thrusting a piece of paper into Eoin's hands.

Among a jumble of numbers and scores, Alan had circled a group of figures in red which read 'Ulster +37, Leinster +16, Connacht -7'.

'What does that mean?' Eoin asked.

'That's the points difference for each of the teams.'

'So?'

'I've checked the regulations on the IRFU website. If two teams are level at the end of the tournament the points difference will decide who wins. So say you win by ten points then Ulster go down to +27, and you go up to +26. Not enough.'

'So we don't just have to beat Ulster, we have to do it by eleven points,' repeated Eoin, slowly coming to understand. 'That makes it an awful lot harder.'

'I know. But it's important that you know that in advance. There'd be nothing worse than winning by ten points and thinking you'd then won the whole thing. That would be such a let-down.'

'We need you in the Leinster set-up Alan, you think of all the important things.'

'Well maybe I could start with Castlerock, as captain you could appoint me Team Analyst, or something like that.'

Eoin laughed and pointed out that although Leinster already had one of them, he'd put a word in with Mr Carey.

'Now, fancy a jog?' he asked, reaching for his kitbag.

The boys headed out to the sports fields to stretch their legs. They trotted alongside each other, chatting more about the game and the likely make-up of the Ireland team when it was all over.

'The Connacht out-half, Joe Kelly, is pretty good,' Eoin mused. He's a better kicker than me, too. I'd be confident of making the match-day twenty-three, but I'm not sure about Paddy O'Hare from Ulster.'

The pair reached the bushes that led to the Rock,

and paused. 'Want to check out if Brian is about?' Eoin asked.

'Yes, please!' grinned Alan. 'I hardly ever get to see ghosts and I haven't seen him for ages.'

Eoin led the way through the bushes, and sure enough there was his spectral pal sitting on the rock. They said their hellos before Eoin asked Brian had he seen Will again.

'Yes, in fact he was around here last night. He was even more agitated than before. He kept muttering about rugby, and repeating the words "Webb Ellis".'

'That's his name!' said Eoin. 'He came to visit me at home.'

'Really,' said Alan, 'You never mentioned that.'

'I forgot it to be honest, the rugby has me distracted. I woke up one night and he was there, looking for something. He was about to tell me why he was here when Dad turned on the light.'

'He doesn't seem dangerous,' said Brian, 'but he's certainly upset about something.'

'Well, if he comes back let him know the fella from Ormondstown was here, will you?'

'I will,' nodded Brian.

'We better get back to our run,' said Eoin, 'I have to be in top condition this weekend.'

CHAPTER 16

Eoin, Alan and Rory got a lift to Belfield on Saturday morning from Mr Carey. The Castlerock coach was keen to meet the Leinster back-room staff and got the boys there three hours before their game was due to kick off. Killian had come from home and was keen to catch up.

'I've never been so nervous in my life before,' he admitted. 'This is even worse than London.'

'I know,' agreed Eoin. 'That just seemed so new and there was no real pressure. This time everyone expects us to win and the World Cup means we're all terrified of making a mistake and missing out.'

'Who's missing out?' came a familiar voice.

'Dylan!' they all echoed.

'Yeah, my email worked!' he grinned. 'The coach rang me last night and asked me to travel up. I'm not in the team, but it'll good to be around them again and who knows what will happen if I get a chance.'

Ted had kept the Leinster selection under wraps all week, but when he gathered his squad together in the dressing room he read out what was undoubtedly the best team he had available.

'From the back, we have Howard, Pedlow, O'Reilly, Horan, McGrath, Madden and Nicholson. And the forwards, from the front, are Nolan, Nolan, Nolan, Muldowney, Farrelly, O'Sullivan, Gill and Bermingham. The organisers have decided we can bring on up to seven replacements from the whole 45 in the squad – so everyone stay loose.'

'He's dropped McCord,' hissed Rory, far more interested in the omission of the second row than his own.

Sure enough, the Dodder Woods bully was turning purple – and was glowering at JD Muldowney who had taken 'his' place.

'Can I have a word, Ted?' McCord interrupted.

'After the game,' snapped the coach.

'But…'

'AFTER the game,' Ted repeated, before turning his back on McCord to talk to Eoin.

McCord sat down, deflated, while everyone else busied themselves and tried to avoid eye contact with him.

Ted quietly ran through his plans with Eoin, and how he saw the replacements panning out. He admitted that he hadn't been sure what to do at scrum-half, where

Rory and Páidí Reeves were also contending for a starting place, but had opted for Killian.

'We'll hit them hard and early, and try to get a good lead up. Their pack is big and strong, but we can beat them if you get the backs moving.'

Eoin nodded and finished off his pre-game routine, tying his left boot before his right and turning his right sock down before his left. Grandad had told him he had similar superstitions, so Eoin had taken them up in his honour. He sometimes got confused about the order, but he didn't take them too seriously.

Ted gave his final pre-match instructions to the team, which were followed to the letter, with Sam Rainey, the Ulster scrum-half, floored by a crunching hit as he took the ball from the first ruck of the game. As Eoin waited for Sam to gather himself to resume, he caught the eye of Paddy O'Hare. To his amusement, his opposite number winked at him. Eoin grinned back, happy that they would all be great friends no matter the result.

Sam lost a bit of confidence from that early hit, and his passing suffered over the next few minutes, allowing Leinster that extra bit of time to intercept, breach the Ulster defence and send Shane Pedlow over for the opening score. Eoin's conversion extended Leinster's lead.

The out-half added three more points in the first-half, slotting over a penalty from outside the twenty-two and winning a thumbs-up from the coach. Eoin noticed that just as Ted had given him the signal he had been tapped on the back by a man wearing a suit – and that the coach then moved away to talk to him.

Ted wasn't on the touchline when the half-time whistle blew and his assistants looked a little confused for about twenty seconds until the coach arrived, flustered.

'Sorry about that, the Leinster chief executive wanted a word with me…'

Ted went through his usual team talk, and suggested some ways of tightening up their play.

'I'm going to make one substitution now. They've got a big scrum and I think we need a bit more power in ours, so I'm going to take off JD and bring on Marcus.'

Eoin's face fell, as did most of the rest of the team. JD was playing a blinder.

'OK, out you go, and keep the scoreboard tilting our way.'

Mention of the scoreboard reminded Eoin to tell the rest of the team that points difference would decide the title, so they had to win by eleven points. Ted's eyes widened and he checked his competition rules booklet.

'Eoin's right, so keep going right to the end,' he told

the team, before taking Eoin aside again.

'That's impressive, Eoin, I wasn't aware of that and I should have been.'

Eoin told him about his pal Alan, and suggested he be made team stats man, which Ted laughed at, but then nodded and said he'd make sure he got a medal if he was the difference between winning and losing.

CHAPTER 17

The introduction of McCord could have proved disastrous. He misread the line-out calls, knocked-on every time he got near the ball, and was yellow carded for using his boot too close to an opponent's head; as the second row jogged to where he had to sit until his ten minutes was up, Ted turned the other way.

During a break in play Eoin was distracted by a huge cheer from the adjoining pitch where the other inter-pro was being played at the same time. He spotted Alan on the sideline and waved at him, pointing towards the cheers.

Alan understood and jogged off to find out what was going on. He returned with a big grin on his face and his thumbs up. Eoin shrugged. Did he mean Munster were winning, or Connacht? Alan drew a large 'C' in the air.

Eoin snorted, 'Typical Leinster fan, wants anyone to win but the Reds,' he thought to himself, before realising which shirt he was wearing.

The Leinster pack came under huge pressure while

McCord was off the field and they eventually cracked. They lost scrum after scrum, but held out with great effort until Sam Rainey slipped through the gap to cross in the corner, bringing the score to 10-5 with ten minutes left.

While the conversion was being taken, and Ted was bringing a new front row on and replacing Killian with Rory, Eoin took the players aside and explained the score difference rule. He told them how they needed to put in much greater effort in the short time that was left.

'You're playing for an Irish cap, remember,' he told them. 'This may be the only time most of us will ever get so close to one. So don't spend your life regretting that you didn't put your all into ten short minutes.'

Luckily, Paddy was off target with the extra-pointer and Leinster kept their five-point lead.

'*If he'd got that we'd need to get eight points to win – which would have meant two scores, which might be too much for us,*' Eoin thought as the team got into position for the game to resume. '*Now it's a try and conversion, or two penalties.*'

Straight from kick off the Leinster forwards barrelled into the opposition with new fire. Panic began to set in with Ulster and a stray hand conceded a penalty just inside the 22, but out on the wing.

'What do you think, Eoin,' asked Rory. 'I've seen you

get much harder ones.'

'I know,' groaned Eoin. 'I'll have to go for it.'

The out-half teed up the ball and took a deep breath. He sized up the kick and swung his leg in rehearsal. He heard another cheer for the neighbouring pitch as he made his run, but put it out of his mind as he concentrated on getting a clean kick in.

Smack! The ball tumbled over itself as it climbed, and as it dropped he was relieved to see both the touch judges raising their flags – 13-5, still three points needed.

By now nearly everyone watching and playing was aware of Alan's calculations, and the Ulster boys were desperate not to make the mistake that would give away a tournament-clinching penalty. Rory took Eoin to one side and cupped his hand to speak into his ear.

'These guys are terrified of giving away a penno. They're backing off tackles. I'm going to try to make a few breaks – will you give me back-up?'

Eoin nodded. Killian was a good, solid scrum-half who delivered the ball quickly and cleanly, but he just didn't have the same attitude as Rory. The Castlerock No 9 was always looking for an opportunity to cause trouble for the opposition and had a good sense for the changes in mood that came throughout a game.

As Leinster crept up the field, every metre was hard

fought. Eoin watched Rory closely, alert to whatever he might be up to. Time was ticking away and because there was no stadium clock, Eoin kept asking the referee how much was left.

'Three minutes,' he replied. 'One minute less than when you last asked.'

'Sorry, ref,' Eoin grinned. 'Just getting a bit nervous.'

The Blues were stuck just inside the Ulster half and getting increasingly frantic in their play.

'Take it easy, lads,' Eoin called out. 'We've all the time we need.'

Rory turned and grinned at him over his shoulder.

As the ball emerged from the ruck the little scrum-half shaped to fling the ball out wide and the Ulster defence moved to make their stand. But Rory hadn't let the ball go, and swivelling on his heel he darted past the wing forward and sidestepped Paddy O'Hare who had been wrong-footed by the move.

Rory tucked the ball under his arm and charged as fast as he could. He zeroed on the goalposts where the only obstacle was the Ulster full-back. 'Where are you, Eoin?' he roared, turning to pass as the last line of defence closed in.

And Eoin was there, as he said he would be, ready to collect the pass, race past the No 15 and touch down under the posts.

The Leinster captain was mobbed by his team but hurried them back to their positions so he could knock over the conversion before facing Ulster's final assault. The Blues held firm however, and there was a huge roar as the whistle sounded for the last time.

There was a strange echo, too, before Eoin realised it had come from the other pitch. Both sides shook hands and some of the Leinster team danced a little jig.

'When do we get the trophy,' asked Rory, as he took the cheers of his team-mates.

'Eh… I'm not sure you will,' gasped Alan, who had just rushed onto the field. He pointed over at the Munster versus Connacht game. 'Connacht are winning… by miles.'

CHAPTER 18

'Oh no!' groaned Eoin. 'But they were miles behind us, weren't they?'

The boys rushed over to the touchline to watch the closing moments.

'It's 46-3' said Alan, I think that means they're five points ahead of you.

He scribbled on his piece of paper which now read 'Ulster +22, Leinster +31, Connacht +36.'

A spectator told them there had been a long break for injury as a Munster winger had broken a leg, so there were still a few minutes left.

Eoin noticed that Dylan had come on as replacement and he gave him a supportive cheer when he made a good tackle.

Dylan looked over and gave them a thumbs up.

The Connacht out-half had signalled for his right winger to go on a run, and he chipped the ball across the field for him to collect. But Dylan had spotted what he was up to and had moved across to cover. He sped in before the ball bounced and snatched it out of the winger's hands.

Eoin grinned, and urged his pal on. He had seventy metres to run – and the shortest legs on the field – but that wasn't going to stop Dylan. Eoin knew he hadn't played for weeks, but he had been working hard on his running every day and Eoin could almost see the extra pace surging through his little legs. He so wanted his pal to do well, and it would be a nice bonus for Leinster too.

Eoin roared Dylan on as he careered along the touch-line, all the while keeping clear of the Connacht defence that had gathered in pursuit. With one last effort, as three boys in green shirts charged towards him, Dylan flung himself into the corner with the ball stretched out in front of him.

'Frrrrrrrrppp!' went the referee's whistle as he lifted his arm straight into the air. The beaten Munster team patted their sole hero on the back as the conversion was taken, but the ball sailed out wide to the left.

'What does that mean, Alan?' gasped Eoin, staring at his friend.

Alan made some more scribbles, and checked the figures again before he spoke.

'It's a tie,' he gulped. 'Leinster +31, Connacht +31'.

Ted wandered across to where the boys were standing, and chuckled as Alan showed him the numbers.

'I'd have taken that a week ago when Connacht beat us. I suppose we'll have to get the chainsaw out for the trophy. I wonder will the Leinster bigwigs mind having a bit of scrap metal in their glass case?'

The tournament organisers called all the teams and spectators together and confirmed that Connacht and Leinster had finished dead level at the top of the table, and as there was no other way of breaking the tie they would share the trophy.

Standing together, Eoin and Joe Kelly awkwardly received the trophy from the IRFU President whose speech thanked them all for playing with such commitment and skill, and wished them well for the forthcoming World Cup.

'And you'll need it,' he grinned. 'The draw was made this morning and I can reveal that your first game is against ....The All Blacks!'

A ripple of laughter went around the ground, but none of the boys moved. No one had been selected yet, and they didn't want to be seen to react to something that might have nothing to do with them.

The President also introduced them to Neil, who would be coaching the Under 16 World Cup team, and told them that the selection committee would be meeting that evening and would send out emails to the lucky thirty-two players as soon as they had picked the squad.

Dylan, Eoin and Rory walked back to the dressing rooms together.

'You do realise you've won the trophy for Leinster,' Eoin ribbed Dylan.

Dylan's mouth opened wide.

'Oh no, I never thought that's what would happen,' he replied, horrified. 'If I'd known that I would have dropped the ball.'

Eoin grinned. 'We'll have to make sure you get a bit of the shrapnel when they cut that cup in half.'

CHAPTER 19

The emails came whizzing into their in-boxes on Monday morning. Mr McCaffrey had allowed the three Castlerock boys who played for Leinster to use the computer room that lunchtime to check their accounts.

Sure enough, Rory, Eoin and Charlie were all delighted to be selected for Ireland, and replied accepting their place in the mini World Cup squad.

Mr Finn called into the common room later to congratulate Eoin.

'I must give Dixie a call too,' he smiled. 'It's a great day for the Madden family as a whole.'

'Tell him I'll call after school,' said Eoin. 'We've lots of work piled on us, it being the first day back.'

The word about the great honour that had been bestowed on the trio spread quickly around the school. Eoin's back was sore from being slapped across it so often, and he got even more embarrassed as each teacher made a point of calling for a round of applause for them before each of the afternoon classes.

After school he walked back to their room with Dylan.

'It's all a bit mad, isn't it?' Eoin laughed. 'Three years ago I'd never played the game and now I'm playing for Ireland.'

'Fair play to you Eoin,' his friend said. 'It's a pity I was out for almost all the interpros. I would have liked to give that a good go.'

'You definitely would have been on,' said Eoin, trying to commiserate. 'Our wingers aren't great – the Connacht lad is strong, but he hasn't got the pace you would have brought.'

Dylan shrugged his shoulders. 'Maybe they'll call me up if there's a few injuries.'

Eoin shook his head. 'Well … Ted told me they were sending emails to the stand-by guys too.'

Dylan stared at him. 'Really? I didn't bother checking because I thought I'd no chance.'

Eoin laughed. 'You're some sap, Dyl. Here, we'll drop over to the computer room, there might be someone there.'

Fifth and Sixth Year boys were allowed use the computers after school and they were given a key to get in and out of the room. Eoin popped his head in the door and found Devin Synnott working at a screen. Devin had been captain of the winning Junior Cup team the year before.

'Hi, lads, what has you up here with the geeks?' he asked.

'Can I check my email?' asked Dylan. 'I'll be quick.'

'Work away, I'm nearly done anyway.'

Dylan logged on to his computer and waited for the mails to arrive. Eoin noticed that his hand was shaking a little.

There was only one email since he'd last logged on, and it bore just four words: 'Irish Rugby Football Union.'

'Yippee!' laughed Eoin, as his friend hurried to open the file.

'Dear Mr Coonan,' it began. *'You have been selected as a stand-by player for the Ireland Under 16 squad to take part in the World Rugby U16 Cup in Dublin. Please read the attached document on the need to maintain your fitness and match practice and reply to this email address stating whether you are available or not.'*

'That's just brilliant!' roared Dylan, drawing a puzzled look from Devin, who was packing his bag.

'Go on, reply,' urged Eoin, 'You're already hours late!'

Dylan wrote back to say 'yes, please' and shut down the computer. The two younger boys waited while Devin locked up.

'How's the rugby going you two?' he asked. 'I heard you're on the Ireland team Eoin – I hope you don't forget we want that Junior Cup back here next year too.'

Eoin grinned. 'No fear of us forgetting that. There's four of us in and around the Irish squad, that's more than any other school in the country. We'll be getting the best of training over the next while so I'm sure we'll be able to turn it on for the likes of St Osgur's and Ligouri College.'

CHAPTER 20

While Dylan went back to the room to tell his pals the news, and to phone his mum, Eoin decided to go for a brisk walk. He was keen to complete his project as early as possible so as to free up time for rugby, and he wanted to get his thoughts in order. He plugged his earphones in, switched on some music, and rambled down towards The Rock.

Eoin liked this part of Castlerock more than any other, and not just because it was where he often met the ghosts. There was an atmosphere about the place that was almost magical, and he found it a good spot to go to think. He burrowed his way through the bushes and came to the clearing beside a tiny stream. He hopped up onto the rock and closed his eyes.

As he worked the project through in his mind, deciding which books he had to read first and which leads to chase up, he heard a rustling among the undergrowth.

'Hello?' he called.

'Young sir?' came the reply, as William appeared in front of him. 'You're the boy from Ormondstown aren't you?' the newcomer asked.

Eoin nodded. 'Yes, and you're William Webb Ellis.'

'Ah yes, you had the book with my story in it. What a strange turn that was.'

Eoin told him he was writing an essay for school about Will's role in the birth of the sport of rugby.

'About me? That's quite extraordinary. What could you possibly find of interest in me?' asked Will.

'Well, the books aren't sure what you did and why the game grew up around the incident. I'd like to ask you a few questions about it…'

'Gosh, it was such a long time ago,' replied Will, 'but fire away.'

Eoin thanked him and paused as he worked out what he needed to know.

'Could you tell me about what Bigside was like as a sport, and maybe tell me some more about what happened on the day you ran?'

Will smiled and began his story. Eoin had a pencil stub in his pocket and started scribbling notes down on the back of a sheet on which he had been selecting his own Ireland Under 16 team.

'It was a rough game, with up to fifty players on each side. Some of the chaps didn't care about the sport, they just saw it as an excuse for some bullying and score-settling. You would often have cracked shins and ankles from playing.

'There weren't many rules of Bigside, but when you caught the ball you could move backwards with it as much as you liked as the other team couldn't come any further than where you had caught it. When that happened a player usually kicked the ball as far as he could, and that's how most goals were scored.

'That day I was too far from goal to try a kick, and the other side seemed a bit disorganised, so I just hared off in the direction of the goal with the ball under my arm. They were so shocked they didn't do anything about it till it was too late and I ran in through the goal.

'I got a fierce ragging from the chaps, and the masters didn't like anyone interfering with one of the great traditions of Rugby School, but after a few days it was all forgotten, or so I thought. I went off to university and played a little cricket, and later joined the Church. I had little time for games then, although I would read the reports in *The Times*. I retired to the west of France and that's where I died and am buried.

'And that's where I thought I would remain for eternity until my spirit was stirred into life some weeks back and I found myself back in Ireland in the very place where I had spent some of my youth.

'It seems to me more than a coincidence that I find myself meeting up with you at your home and now at your school. Perhaps you could be the key to the mystery of why I have come…'

Another rustling sound came from the bushes, and Eoin turned to see Dylan climbing through.

'How are ya, Eoin, I thought I might find you here,' he grinned.

Eoin turned back around, but found the ghostly pioneer of rugby had disappeared.

'Ah Dyl! That was bad timing. He was just about to tell me why he was here…'

'Who?' asked Dylan.

'William… I've found another ghost, or rather *he's* found *me*. He invented rugby.'

'Is he the lad that Dixie was telling us about?'

'Yeah, he came to see me in Ormondstown, and now he's turned up here. I'm doing my project about him so it's been pretty useful. He's very upset about something and I think he was just about to tell me when you came barging in.'

Dylan shrugged. 'Sorry buddy, but I can't keep track of all your dealings with the spirit world. Now, fancy going for a jog? I have some serious fitness programme to get through just to be on standby.'

Eoin sighed and tucked his notes into his pocket. Dylan was a great friend but he did have a habit of turning up when he wasn't needed.

Later, back in the dorm, Alan was the most excited of them all, despite being the only resident who wasn't about to be sized up for a green jersey.

'This is so cool!' he gurgled. 'Three Irish internationals and the hero of Leinster's joint interpro win. We are officially the most talented dorm in all of Castlerock.'

'Hero of *what*?' laughed Dylan.

'Well if it wasn't for my skill with addition and subtraction those Connacht lads would be champions,' sniffed Alan.

'You did indeed play an important role,' grinned Eoin, 'but to call yourself the *hero*...'

'Yeah, it was my break and killer pass that set up the try, not your stubby pencil and paper,' chuckled Rory.

Alan frowned. 'Oh well, I'm sorry you don't appreciate my efforts...'

'Hang on, hang on,' laughed Eoin. 'I just said you *did* play an important role, but we still had to score the points out on the pitch.'

'All right, Al,' laughed Dylan. 'I'll give the IRFU a

shout and get them to organise you a special green and white calculator, and maybe a pencil set.'

'Would you?' asked Alan earnestly. 'And maybe an official hoodie too?'

Dylan roared with laughter.

'I will not, you eejit,' he laughed. 'I'm barely getting a shirt myself.'

Eoin grinned at Alan. 'Look, your calculations were brilliant, and they definitely helped. I'll ask Ted can you have a role with Leinster – maybe keeping note of who plays for how many minutes, and who scores, kicking percentages and all that. All the big teams have a guy to do that for them.'

'That would be amazing,' said Alan. 'I sort of do all that anyway,' he added as he produced a notebook full of numbers and names.

Eoin riffled through the book, astonished at the detail Alan had gathered on all the games he had watched.

'Here, what's my place kick percentage?' he asked.

'Off the top of my head … 91 per cent inside the 22 metre line, 65 per cent outside. And 0 per cent inside the opposition half.'

'Ah, but that was a tactical move,' laughed Eoin, remembering the crucial last play in the European final at Twickenham the summer before. 'And we scored from it!'

CHAPTER 21

The boys in what Alan continued to call 'the most talented dorm in Castlerock' were kept busy over the next few weeks. Every Sunday morning was spent at Ireland training, but they also had to complete a daily programme of stretching exercises and sprints with a five kilometre jog every second day. The school's Junior Cup team had training three afternoons a week, as well as games once a week. Fitting in school work was hard going for Eoin and his pals, but the teachers made sure they didn't slip back.

Eoin was keen to finish the history project before the Under 16 World Cup kicked off, but soon realised that he had little chance of doing so. William's explanation of how Bigside worked was very useful, but he needed to get some more details on what Rugby School was like at the time, and what William had done with his life. He also wanted to know what William remembered of Ormondstown.

But every time Eoin swung by The Rock the rugby pioneer was nowhere to be seen.

'I haven't seen him for weeks, Eoin,' said Brian, who appeared at The Rock one Saturday morning. 'He was in a very strange mood when I last saw him. I tried to ask him to explain what he was doing here but he cut me short. Quite rude he was, to be honest.'

Eoin sighed. 'I know what you mean. He's an odd fellow, but perhaps people behaved differently two hundred years ago.'

Brian grinned. 'I'm over one hundred years old!' he chuckled.

'I know, I know,' spluttered Eoin. 'No offence, honestly, but you've spent a lot of time with people in the twenty-first century so you know how we do things nowadays…'

Brian laughed out loud. 'OK, Eoin, stop digging. William is just a bit odd. He's very preoccupied with something and maybe he doesn't trust us enough to share it just yet. If and when that happens, he will. So don't worry about things you can't have any influence on and concentrate on things you do – so tell me what's happening with this Irish rugby team…'

Eoin nodded in agreement.

'Well the tournament is coming up fast – the last full training session is tomorrow, then the opening ceremony is on Friday. We play next Saturday morning. Will you be floating along?'

'I might just,' laughed Brian.

'We've a decent team, some excellent players when you put them all together. Over the last few weeks Neil has had us going through all the moves and assessing what we need to work on. We haven't even played a practice match, which has slightly concerned me as we don't know how he's thinking about selection. I really hope we have one tomorrow.'

CHAPTER 22

Eoin got his wish. It was a frosty morning when the final training session began and, after the usual stretches and exercises, Neil called the group together.

'Right lads, thank you all for coming today and this is the last time we'll all be together as the final 32 will have to break off for the tournament. I've invited along all the players I asked to be on standby, and I will probably be promoting one or two into the full squad as I'm unhappy with the fitness commitment shown by some of you. Today will tell a lot on that score.'

Eoin looked across to Dylan who was trying not to grin but had a most determined look on his face.

'We're going to measure and test you first, then break into sectors and go through some moves. But this afternoon I've invited along a school side to play you in a practice match,' explained Neil. 'I'll tell you more about that after lunch.'

After the bombshell about late changes to the squad the training session was a nervy affair.

'It's like a trial all over again,' gasped Sam during a

short break.

'I know,' replied Eoin, 'You can see how some lads have got very nervous.'

'I've dropped the ball twice,' groaned Killian, 'I'd say I'm in trouble.'

At lunch – two bananas and a bottle of water – Neil addressed the troops.

'Right, first of all I'm going to announce a team that will start the game at 2.15pm. We see this as the likely starting team to face New Zealand, and we will allow you to play for at least an hour as a unit today before we bring on any replacements. Having said that, there are still quite a few positions where we aren't 100 per cent certain so don't be complacent if you're in the first XV, and don't be downhearted if you're not.'

Neil read the team out: 'Backs … Peak, Nowak, O'Hare, Bourke, McGrath, Madden, Rainey. And the forwards … Nolan, Brady, Young, Savage, Savage, Deegan, Bermingham, Steenson.'

There was a gasp when he read the name of the first prop out, as James Nolan from Dunboyne had previously been a standby player. All eyes turned to the boy who everyone was sure would be the loose-head.

'OK, so you will have noticed we've made a big change,' explained Neil. 'And while I'm sorry to have to do it, we did set reasonable fitness targets which weren't met. James has impressed me today and I'm now sure we have the best front row possible.'

Adam, the boy who had been dropped, bit his lip and bowed his head. Eoin was gutted for him as he was one of the friendliest in the squad, but he had noticed that he wasn't keeping up with the pace.

'The game will be kicking off shortly, and we're taking on a schools' team from Dublin. They're nothing special, I believe, but they're bigger and heavier than you, which will give you some idea of what awaits you with the New Zealanders.'

Neil pointed behind the boys, where the opposition was warming up. They were wearing black shorts but also had some familiar green and white shirts and, to Eoin, there were a few familiar faces.

Devin Synnott gave him a wave.

'We're playing the Castlerock College senior cup team,' announced Neil. 'So give it your best.'

CHAPTER 23

Eoin gulped. The Castlerock team were two, some even three, years older than the Ireland boys and most of the pack towered over even the Savage brothers.

'This is a bad idea,' muttered Paddy. 'They'll kill us.'

'They're no great shakes as a team,' Eoin told them. 'But they're very physical. Keep your wits about you at all times.'

Neil called his squad back for one last announcement. 'Also, I've decided to go outside the provincial captains for this team as I want to go with someone who I'm certain will be a first choice and play all the games. I've been impressed with his leadership all season and want you all to give your full support to Charlie Bermingham.'

Eoin stopped dead in his tracks. He was delighted for Charlie, but what did Neil mean when he said he wanted someone who was certain to be a first choice? Was his place in danger? But to who? It had to be the Connacht out-half, Joe Kelly. He hadn't faced any serious rivals for his place in any team since soon after he took up rugby.

Charlie looked shocked as he turned to Eoin.

'Captain? Me? I can't even tie my shoelaces without checking on YouTube. He's got to be joking.'

'No way,' said Eoin. 'You're a leader, everyone says that. You know how to get the guys going and everyone looks up to you. I'll work with you on the calls but take it with both hands and enjoy it.'

'This is so wrong Eoin,' said Charlie. 'What does he mean, is he going to drop you?'

'I don't know, it was as much a shock to me,' he admitted.

The referee blew the whistle to get the players settled and they all moved into position ready for Eoin to kick off.

The ball hung in the air while the Ireland forwards chased its path. Oisín Deegan leapt to collect it, but was floored by a huge Castlerock prop who crashed into him as he fell.

'Whoa!' called the ref, who instantly blew his whistle. 'This is a friendly match, organised to help warm up these boys who will represent Ireland next week. That was a dangerous move and if it was a proper match you would be cooling your heels on the sideline for ten minutes,' he nodded at the Castlerock prop.

'Now cool it down and remember why you're here. Any sign of aggro and you'll be off. We don't want any unnecessary injuries.'

Eoin's face didn't move, but he smiled inside with gratitude at the referee's good sense.

And as Eoin had said earlier, The Castlerock boys weren't a very good side. Neil was happy that the forwards were getting a good testing, losing most of the set-plays to their bigger, heavier opponents (although the giant Savage brothers did their best to compete) but redressing the balance by battling well in the rucks.

Sam was a bit loose in delivering the ball out to Eoin, who therefore had less time to get it moving than he had with Rory at scrum-half. He liked Sam a lot, but he hoped Neil had noticed this and would make the obvious change.

The Ireland side had two seriously quick wingers – Kuba Nowak from Connacht and Ollie McGrath, who Eoin had played against a couple of times when Castlerock met Belvedere. With such pace, it was important to give them as many chances as they could to score so Eoin got his backs running regularly and played some neat cross kicks, which led to a try apiece.

At half-time Eoin got a pat on the back each from Kuba and Ollie, and the team were buzzing from the battle which they were leading easily.

'OK, don't get too excited you lot,' grinned Neil. 'As I said they're nothing special and I expect you to run in some more tries as the game goes on. We've battled well up front and I was especially happy with the way James fitted in.

'But, Eoin, you'll need to get the ball away a lot quicker against New Zealand,' snapped Neil. 'The Castlerock wing-forwards are slow, but you can be sure they won't be next weekend.'

Eoin was stunned at the criticism, but just nodded. He couldn't complain about Sam – but to be blamed for the slow ball really annoyed him.

CHAPTER 24

Eoin was still grumbling to himself when the second half kicked off, but he tried to fight the negative feelings that he had. He was convinced he would be replaced shortly and became even more desperate to improve and impress the coach.

Sam, too, sensed there was a need to perform better and was certainly a lot faster getting the ball back from the first ruck of the second half. Unfortunately, Eoin was so preoccupied that he lost concentration for a moment and the ball slipped from his grasp and he knocked it forwards.

As the scrum formed Eoin glanced across to the touch-line where he saw Joe Kelly stripping off his tracksuit.

He slapped his thigh and warned himself to concentrate. He needed to make the most of what little time he might have left to keep his place.

Oisín Deegan was quick off the mark and collared the Castlerock scrum-half before he could get the ball away. The Ireland pack swarmed around him and Charlie Bermingham funnelled the ball back to Sam. The scrum-half took a dart to his left but as he was tackled he turned and fired the ball straight and true into Eoin's hands.

With the extra second or two his team-mate had earned him, Eoin set off on a break, beating two men before he offloaded to Paddy O'Hare who was playing in the centre. The Ulsterman was just as quick-witted and slipped the ball out to Kuba who stormed past the last of the defenders to score.

The Ireland players swarmed all over the winger, delighted that so many of the team had contributed to such an excellent try.

'Great break, Eoin,' came a call from the sideline as Eoin prepared to take the conversion.

Eoin looked across and saw Alan jumping up and down wearing a green and white bobble hat. He smiled to himself and thought how he would always have one die-hard supporter, no matter what.

'You've great support there – and here,' came a voice from behind him, and Eoin whirled around to see Brian Hanrahan standing there, his black, red and yellow hooped shirt making him look out of place on a field where only the referee wasn't wearing a combination of green and white.

'Concentrate on this kick and then get yourself back

in the game quickly,' Brian said. 'Neil thinks you're the best out-half but some of the other coaches are in his ear about the Connacht lad. Just show them you're the man.'

Eoin slotted the ball over easily, and the scoreboard showed that there was no real chance of the Castlerock side making a comeback.

Eoin was terrified to look towards the touchline as he waited for play to restart. The Castlerock No 10 overdid his kick and the ball came comfortably to Roger Savage, who turned and found Sam. The scrum-half flipped it on to Eoin who had spotted that Ollie McGrath had his hand in the air on the far wing. He hoisted the ball across the pitch, where it tumbled down towards Ollie, who plucked it from the air and ran unchallenged under the posts with his arm still aloft.

There was a huge roar from the touchline as all the squad members and coaching stuff cheered what every-one said was a brilliant move.

When Neil called Eoin ashore a few minutes later as part of a large reshuffle the young out-half wasn't put out at all. He knew he had made an important point and could now be reasonably certain that he would be starting against the Baby Blacks.

Joe Kelly and Rory Grehan came on as the new

half-back combination and did OK, but Castlerock were fading badly and surely Neil would take that into account, hoped Eoin.

'Thanks, lads,' said Neil as they wound down the day's activities. 'Now there's only six days to the first game and we won't be getting together till the day before. Keep working hard at your fitness and your drills.'

Eoin packed his bag and walked out to the car-park, where the Castlerock bus was parked.

'Any chance of lift, lads?' he grinned, as he led Charlie, Rory and Dylan aboard.

He took a few hits from rolled-up socks – and a stream of slagging from Devin Synnott – but no harm was done and they were soon back at the school.

CHAPTER 25

The rest of the week was spent in a blur. Every teacher wished the Castlerock contingent well and every time Eoin wandered out of a classroom there was a first-year wanting him to sign an autograph book. He didn't mind that at all, but he got very fed up of the constant request for selfies.

When school finished for the Christmas holidays on Thursday Eoin, Charlie and Rory packed up their bags and headed down with Dylan to the headmaster's office to where they had been invited. The rugby coaches were there waiting for them.

'This is such a fantastic honour for the school,' smiled Mr Finn. 'We've never had as many as three men in the green shirt at one time before at any level ... and with a fourth man in readiness in case he's needed. You've done yourselves and the school proud.'

The headmaster added his own words of praise and Eoin struggled to keep his smile fixed as the fourth and fifth speeches in their honour floated by his ears. The headmaster presented them all with a special school tie and they all then tucked into sandwiches and drinks before Mr Carey called the boys aside.

'Right lads, we'll have to leave shortly. I've promised the IRFU I'll deliver you to Belfield for six o'clock and traffic will be heavy. Drink up and make your farewells.'

Dylan was a little grumpy as he saw them off. 'Give that Ollie fella a kick any chance you get,' he sniffed. 'I'll try to get down to watch the games anyway.'

'Look, Dyl, if half of what they say about these New Zealanders is true then we'll all be stretchered off and you'll be warming up at half-time. Just do what Neil said and keep the fitness programme going.'

Dylan grinned. 'I'm sure I could play out-half if you, Paddy and the Connacht lad are all crocked.'

Eoin wagged a finger at his pal. 'You've more chance of playing prop,' he called through the window as the car pulled away.

Mr Carey got them to the Leinster Rugby HQ just in time, and the boys lifted their kitbags out of his boot and thanked him before he drove off. Inside the hall there was the same array of shirts, bags and training tops as he had seen in the summer, but this time the blue had turned to green and there was green blazer hanging on a hook with each boy's name written on an attached piece of card.

116

Eoin collected his kit, swopping banter with Ollie McGrath as they lugged the heavy bags into the middle of the hall.

After a speech of welcome from an IRFU official, a man from World Rugby who called himself Fitzy also talked to them about the competition and what was expected of them. He handed them each a book-let about the event, which included a timetable that told Eoin where he needed to be every fifteen minutes for the next week. They also got a plastic card to hang around their neck which told the world that they were a 'PLAYER' at the World Rugby U-15 World Cup. Eoin stared at his photo and realised just what it meant to be there.

After more mini-lectures – including one from Neil – they were told to find their name on the list of bed-rooms at the back of the hall, and to meet up for break-fast at 7.45am.

Eoin found he had been billeted with Paddy O'Hare, James Brady and Jarlath Vasey, a good mixture from all over the country. He liked Paddy a lot, and the other two seemed good lads too. They were all exhausted, especially those who had had to travel a good distance, and there was little chat before they all settled down for the night.

117

Eoin woke during the night with a nagging pain in his head. He got up for a drink and stood at the window while he sipped from the bottle. The building over-looked the sports fields, which were lit by the moon. And there he spotted, walking quickly, a white figure with old-fashioned shoes topped with a shiny buckle that glinted in the moonlight. As the figure strode on, seemingly searching for something, he suddenly stopped and turned to stare straight at Eoin in the window.

He mouthed something at him, but as soon as it escaped from his lips he disappeared. Eoin was disturbed at the clearly agitated vision, but even more so by what he thought had said. He couldn't be certain, but William seemed to be asking him for 'Help'.

CHAPTER 26

There was a small, low-key opening ceremony for the tournament ahead of the opening fixture at the Belfield Bowl, which proved more irritating than exciting for Eoin. With the most important game of his career less than an hour away, the last thing he wanted to be doing was marching around a rugby field with nearly three hundred and fifty other lads and standing listening to speeches.

As he suppressed a yawn his eye caught a boy three rows in front who was wearing a bright yellow blazer, and seemed to be waving. But who was he waving at?

'Eoin,' he heard the boy hiss. The stranger's head was completely shaved, but something about him was familiar.

'Who … is that … Charlie?' he eventually realised.

'Yes!' came the reply, with a thumbs-up. 'Catch you later!'

Charlie Johnston was a team-mate at Castlerock until the summer before, when he and his family emigrated to Australia. He had obviously made a quick return though, as a member of the Under 16 Wallabies.

'Does that make him a Joey?' Eoin wondered to himself.

He shuffled from one foot to the other, impatient for the ceremonies to be over so he could prepare for the game. The Irish and New Zealand sides were allowed to wear tracksuits, under which they wore their match kit, while the rest of the countries wore suits or blazers. The tournament timetable also told them they could leave the ceremony with thirty minutes to kick off, and Eoin was relieved when Charlie got the nod from Neil to lead his side off and back to the dressing rooms.

The Ireland fifteen that started against Castlerock was unchanged and Eoin sat beside Sam to chat about their moves and signals.

Neil gave them a final run-through, but he told them that all their work was done, now all they needed to do was follow the plans and show off their skills as the best fifteen rugby players of their age in the country.

Eoin caught a glimpse of himself in a mirror, and was a bit taken aback to realise that he was wearing that famous green jersey with white shamrocks sprouting across his chest. It was the first time the significance of what he had done was brought home to him.

'Wow,' he said to himself. 'Picked for Ireland at a sport

you had never even played three years ago…'

He put that thought out of his mind and joined the queue of players heading for the door. He nodded to Rory, who was one of the replacements, and followed Charlie as he trotted out onto the field at the head of the Irish team.

Eoin took one look to his left as they did so and was astonished to see how big their opponents looked. His grandad had warned him that the New Zealanders used their all-black kit to intimidate opponents, and that psychologists said it made them look bigger than they were. But there was no getting away from it: Ireland were going to need to find a way to win this game that didn't involve height and strength.

Eoin also noticed that some of his team-mates were looking rattled already. He went over and shook Noah by the shoulders and reminded him of how quick and battling he had been in the interpros, and how it was those skills that would help Ireland most. Noah grinned back at him and nodded.

The stands at the university ground were full, and the green banners and replica shirts swamped all the others. He waved to his parents – and his grandfather Dixie – and mouthed a 'thanks for coming' to them.

There was a huge cheer after they sang 'Ireland's Call',

and every Irish player's name was greeted with a shout of support. To hear his name called out – and cheered – gave Eoin a tingle up his spine.

As the teams lined up in formation before the kick off, Eoin glanced over to the front of the stand and saw that a little platform had been erected on which sat two trophies. One was the Under 16 World Cup trophy, a picture of which was on their identity cards, but it was the other cup that knocked Eoin out of his stride. Was that what was causing William to be so worried? Hadn't he mentioned it when they first met back in his bedroom in Ormondstown?

Sitting on the table, shining in the winter sunlight, was the prize awarded to the winners of the senior men's Rugby World Cup.

The William Webb Ellis Cup.

CHAPTER 27

Eoin didn't have any more time to think about the trophy, or William, as the referee's whistle blew and the New Zealand out-half kicked the ball towards the lines of forwards converging to his left.

Roger Savage leapt to gather the ball, but was taken out of the air by a barrelling Kiwi forward.

The referee blew his whistle, signalling a penalty to Ireland.

Roger was flat out, and as he was helped to his feet Eoin could see he was dazed.

The medic signalled to Neil that he would need to send on a replacement.

'No card?' asked Sam, astonished.

The referee turned away.

'They never send anyone off this early,' grinned the Kiwi captain. 'It's a free hit, basically.'

Eoin was appalled that anyone would go out to do damage to an opponent, and to do it for such a cynical reason only made it worse.

Roger was helped from the field as the big second row

from Connacht came on to replace him. Jarlath Vasey wasn't as good a player as Roger, but he was bigger and stronger.

Eoin kicked the penalty into the corner and jogged over to take his place in the set-piece.

'These arrogant Kiwis need to be taken down,' Sam smiled, before whispering a plan into Eoin's ear.

Eoin held up four fingers to the backs – code for one of their moves – and awaited the line out. Vasey made an initial impact, his extra height allowing him to compete with the All Blacks and he caught the ball cleanly and the ruck formed around him as he returned to earth.

The New Zealand power began to tell as Ireland were driven back a couple of metres, but the ball came out to Sam who flipped it on to Eoin.

Facing the right wing, Eoin swivelled on his heels and chipped the ball delicately towards the opposite corner. The defence was caught on the wrong foot and were stunned to see Ollie McGrath charging down the left wing like a turbo-powered cheetah.

As the ball bobbled towards the touchline, Ollie scooped it up and took one step inside before diving over the try-line to score Ireland's first points of the tournament.

There was an enormous roar as the Ireland supporters

who packed the stands were carried away with delight.

Eoin and Sam exchanged huge grins, overjoyed that their plan to replay the try against Castlerock the previous weekend had come off so well.

The roar echoed as Eoin added the two points and he smiled as the scoreboard sprang to life to show 'Ireland 7 New Zealand 0'.

But the setback only seemed to make Ireland's opponents even more determined and their greater strength and power began to tell. One of the Kiwi props went on a forty-metre run that took him close to Ireland's try-line, and a slick handling move between the back-row forwards saw them score under the posts. Another try before half-time left Ireland trailing by five points.

'Forget the score, that was an excellent first-half,' said Neil. 'I'm very proud of how you stood up to the early set-back. Brilliant try, Ollie, and a very clever move Eoin. It's that sort of quick-thinking and skill that will allow us to compete with their strength. Keep it up.'

However, it got harder and harder to absorb the heavy hits of the powerful New Zealanders, some of whom had the physiques of grown men. Eoin went through the plays Neil had suggested, but the Kiwis were able to soak up most of them. Neil emptied the bench of all his forward options, but still Ireland found it hard to break through. Eoin's kicking kept them in the game, and the score display unit blinked out '19-13' as the clock ticked into the last minute.

New Zealand were controlling a ruck around half-way, but Oisín Deegan was still prepared to battle all the way. He drove into the pile of bodies, and emerged with the ball in hand. The momentum was with Ireland and Sam fired the ball out to Eoin who spotted the Kiwi backs were a bit disorganised.

He thumped the ball high into the air towards the wing and charged after it. He arrived just as the Garry-owen returned from its trip to the clouds and gathered it in his hands. He had a clear run to the line and made for it, but as he dived he was hit by what seemed like an iron rhinoceros.

Seconds later he opened his eyes and was alarmed to see the faces above swirling in a jumble of features.

'Are you OK, Eoin?' asked Sam.

'I… I… I don't know' replied Eoin.

'Lie still son, we'll have you checked,' said the referee, which made Eoin even more worried that he had been injured.

The doctor came over to him and checked him before asking him his name and age, and to count her fingers.

'OK, I'll take you off, you seem fine, but there's only

a few seconds left so it's best to be safe,' said the medic.

Eoin was helped onto a stretcher and he stared at the clouds as he was carried from the field.

'Who's going to take the conversion,' he heard Kuba call, only then realising that he had scored a try.

'Will you take it, Joe?' asked Charlie, tossing the ball to Eoin's replacement.

Joe was only just on the field and hadn't expected to be facing such a crucial kick. With the score at 19-18 to New Zealand and a huge crowd waiting for his conversion the pressure got to him.

As Eoin was lifted into the ambulance he heard the crowd let out a huge sigh, followed by a tiny cheer, which greeted the long whistle to signal full-time.

CHAPTER 28

Eoin lay on a trolley in the ambulance and checked his shoulders and arms for signs of pain. The ambulance had not pulled away yet, and people kept coming to check on him.

His mum and dad called in, too, anxious and concerned, but relieved that he was in good hands.

'OK, son, we'll take you away to get checked,' said the ambulance man as he dropped his holdall under the bed on which Eoin lay. He kicked it in further against the wall and disappeared again to start the vehicle.

'Is he concussed?' asked his worried mother.

The ambulance man returned a blank look. 'Eh, eh,' he stammered. 'I wouldn't be able to tell you that. But they'll do all the tests in the hospital.'

The Ireland doctor hopped in just then, and explained a little more to the Maddens about what would be happening. She chatted away to Eoin as the ambulance drove him at high speed to the nearest hospital, wincing as the vehicle took a sharp series of bends and speed bumps.

'We lost, didn't we?' Eoin asked the doctor.

'Yes, Joe just missed the conversion. It's a pity as it was a brilliant performance to stay so close to them,' she replied.

'Will I be OK for the next game?' asked Eoin.

'That depends on what they say here. We'll have to keep an eye on you for a day or two to check you haven't been concussed. But if you have been then you can't play for twenty-three days.'

'Twenty-three days! But… that's long after the final!'

'I'm sorry, but that's the way it has to be. Concussion can be very dangerous and we need to be sure you're one hundred per cent before you can return to play.'

Eoin bit his lip and was relieved that the ambulance had arrived at the hospital.

He was taken in and examined by another doctor, and after an X-ray he was admitted to a single room – still wearing his Ireland gear. All evening he was poked and prodded and a nurse kept checking his temperature and pulse, before the IRFU doctor returned to say they were happy with him, but would keep him overnight for observation.

'Roger Savage is in the next ward so I'll call by to see him. Now I'll let your mum and dad in to see you. A couple of your pals begged me to bring them along so

129

I'll let them up to talk to you for five minutes too. And then try to sleep.'

His parents came in and the doctor explained what had happened and what needed to be done.

'You were lucky you had an ambulance and doctor there so quickly,' said his dad. 'And the hospital so close by.'

His mum fussed over him and told him to be careful, but they had to go home that night as Dixie had a doctor's appointment early next morning.

'I'll give you a ring tomorrow and see if I can visit,' said his dad.

His parents said goodbye and soon after that the doctor left. A minute later the door opened slowly and Alan and Dylan peeped in.

'Thanks for coming, lads, but where's the grapes and Lucozade?'

Alan looked embarrassed, but Dylan laughed.

'Grapes! You're having a laugh. What's the grub like here?'

'Grub? So far it's been toast and tea. I think I arrived too late and the kitchen was closed.'

'Shame about the result,' said Dylan.

'Yeah, we were so close. I really thought we could win the World Cup.'

'Well, we still can,' Alan replied.

'Really? How come?' asked Eoin. 'Surely New Zealand will win our group now?'

'Yes, but it's three groups of three teams – the winners get into the semi-finals but the best loser does too. It will come down to points difference and we're only minus one point. A good win over Italy and we've a great chance to be in the semis.'

Eoin grinned. Alan was much better at the details than he was.

'I should have read that tournament handbook they gave us,' he laughed before suddenly becoming serious. 'I hope they let me play – it could be more than three weeks if the doctors say so.'

Right on cue the IRFU medic poked her head around the door and signalled Eoin's friends it was time to go.

'By the way, the tournament was the main item on the television news just now,' she told the boys.

'Really? Because of Eoin's injury? Or was it the result?' asked Dylan.

'No, of course not. Didn't you hear? Someone walked off with one of the trophies. It's terribly embarrassing for the IRFU. There's a huge Garda search going on out at the grounds – the World Cup – the big one – has been stolen.'

CHAPTER 29

Eoin was stunned by the news. He realised that this was what William's appearance had been all about. And he should have known when he saw the Webb Ellis trophy sitting on the platform before the game.

'I should have warned someone,' he said, aloud.

'Why?' asked the doctor.

Eoin stopped, realising this was not something he could explain away easily.

'I had a dream that it was stolen,' he spluttered.

The doctor looked at him suspiciously.

'Really? A dream?'

'Yes. I know it sounds stupid, but I sometimes I have very vivid dreams. The trophy kept appearing in them and then when I saw it before the game I should have realised why.'

'That's a weird coincidence, but I don't think you will have to explain that to the Guards,' grinned the doctor. 'Now, lights out and try to sleep.'

When they had all left Eoin stared at the ceiling. It wasn't long before William Webb Ellis appeared. He

132

looked very upset.

'Eoin, what on *earth* has happened?' he asked.

'Your guess is as good as mine, Will,' Eoin replied. 'I was playing the match and didn't hear about the trophy until just now. Were you there?'

William nodded. 'I watched that game – though it's hard to imagine how they could ever have said I invented it – and saw the trophy with my own eyes. It was then I realised my presence must have had something to do with it so I kept a keen eye out. Unfortunately, I was distracted – and not a little concerned – when you were injured. The trophy must have been stolen around that time.'

Eoin frowned. 'I'm amazed there was no one in charge of watching the cup.'

'There *was*,' replied William. 'But he was called away to find the key for the gate because the ambulance man wanted to take you around to a different entrance. He said it was quicker that way.'

'This is awful,' said Eoin. 'I'm sure the IRFU will be very embarrassed too.'

'I will go back there now and try to investigate,' said William. 'Perhaps when the medicine men are finished with you, you will join me?'

Eoin agreed and bade farewell to William. He lay back

on the bed but it took ages to get to sleep.

Next morning Eoin had to undergo all the tests again, and then returned to his room to await the doctors' verdict. He called in to see Roger Savage and the pair joked at the unlikelihood of two lads from Ormondstown playing rugby for Ireland, let alone being carted off to hospital during the same game.

'When you got injured did you get the same ambulance as me?' asked Roger. 'A big yellow one? I'm only asking as the driver had to stop on the way here to throw up. It was just outside the back gate, but he was in agony and had to ring to get someone else to collect us. He came in the back with me and the doctor said it looked like he had eaten something poisonous. Poor man.'

Eoin frowned. 'Now that you mention it, I was in a white ambulance. They must have had to call up a replacement after your driver went sick.'

The boys went back to talking about the tournament, although Roger was downbeat about his chances of playing again.

'The docs said I was concussed. They want to keep me here for a couple more days. No more rugby for me till after Christmas. I just hope Neil lets me stay with the squad for the rest of the tournament.'

Eoin bid farewell to Roger and returned to his room, where a doctor was busy studying his X-rays and scans.

'Right, young man, I have good news. You got a bit of a heavy bang and a little bit of bruising, but it looks like you escaped the worst of it. I'm going to recommend you sit out the next game but you will ready to play again in about a week. I've called the IRFU doctor and she'll be around to collect you shortly.'

CHAPTER 30

Eoin was glad to rejoin the Irish squad and although they were disappointed to lose their opening game, Alan had explained the system to them so they were determined to qualify for the semi-finals.

'We'll have to keep an eye on the other groups to make sure we know our opposition,' said Alan, 'but I'd say we have a great chance.'

He laid out the tournament programme on the table in front of Eoin.

'Pool B is tough – England, Wales and Australia, while Pool C is France, Scotland and South Africa. It's hard to tell who to watch out for as none of these teams have ever played together before, but you've got to expect England, Australia and South Africa to be very strong. That's why that last try against the Kiwis could be crucial – our points difference is as good as it can be with a defeat!'

Eoin grinned. Alan could always be relied on to look on the bright side of life.

'Let's check out the opposition later – there's a couple

of games today down at the Bowl,' Eoin suggested. 'But first I have to check in with Neil.'

Eoin talked to the coach, and the doctor, who told him he wasn't allowed to train for a day or two, but gave him a few suggestions to keep his fitness levels up. He liked the sound of cycling, and thought it would be a good way to explore the vast university complex where they were based.

After arranging to borrow a bicycle, Eoin set off to do a lap of the grounds to help get his bearings. With lots of roundabouts and one-way roads he found it very complicated, and after a while he was so bored he was about to give up. He found himself back at the gate of the tournament venue – the same gate the ambulance driver had decided wasn't near enough to the hospital.

Eoin cycled out the entrance into the roadway and was astonished to realise that just a few metres away he could see the giant telecoms pylon that stood over the national television station.

He was puzzled. He had seen this several times before, usually on his occasional visits to hospital to visit his grandad or have some rugby injury patched up. He cycled down the road and sure enough, there were the familiar buildings that housed the broadcaster.

He pushed the bicycle across the busy road at the pedestrian lights and jumped back into the saddle to freewheel down the hill. A minute or so later the huge hospital loomed into view.

Eoin stopped and scratched his head. It had taken him barely two minutes to get from the ground to the hospital on a bicycle and on foot. Why did the ambulance driver see the need to go another way, which involved waiting for the key to be found, then taking some sharp turns and speed bumps for what had seemed like ten minutes when he could have driven straight down the hill?

The mystery annoyed him too, as the whole point of ambulances is to get a sick or injured person to hospital as quickly as possible – messing like that could have been very dangerous in a different situation.

He cycled back up to the campus where the next game was about to start. He found Alan sitting on the grass with his notebook.

'I'm keeping an eye on the opposition, taking down stats of what they do with the ball. I think I'd like to do this for school, too.'

Eoin grinned. 'Thanks, Al, that could be really useful.' He turned to look at the game being played out on the pitch.

'Oh there's Charlie Johnston – that gold shirt suits him well. It's amazing he got onto the team so quickly.'

'Not really,' replied Alan. 'He told me he got a good introduction from Ted to the Australian rugby union so they had their eye on him from the minute he got over there. Charlie says they're not a bad side but their out-half can't kick so they don't expect to win.'

Charlie was right about the out-half. The only kicks he converted were when his team scored under the posts, but happily for Australia there were a few of them. They were far too strong for Wales, winning 31-7, with Charlie running in two of the tries.

CHAPTER 31

While they waited for the second game they chatted about the missing trophy. There were still several Gardaí running around asking questions and taking photographs. The podium with the Under 16 World Cup sitting upon it was still in place, but this time with no fewer than three security men standing guard.

'Where were they all when the trophy went missing?' laughed Alan as the trio in uniform folded their arms in unison and glared at anyone that stopped to look at the trophy.

There were other spectators within hearing distance, so Eoin signalled to Alan to join him up higher on the bank well away from anyone else's ears.

'This robbery is terrible, Alan. It looks really bad for Ireland – and worse, I sort of knew about it in advance,' he told his friend. 'I had a visit at home from a lad called William – William Webb Ellis. Him who invented rugby.'

Alan's eyes bulged. 'Really? Webb Ellis? The guy they named the trophy after?'

'Yes,' answered Eoin. 'He just appeared one night and

was all upset, but he didn't know why. I think he must have had some inkling about the trophy without knowing. He visited me in the hospital and he is completely distraught about it. I think he sees this cup as his connection to the sport he invented.'

'But you couldn't have known that the trophy was going to be stolen...'

'As soon as I saw it on that stand over there I knew that was why William had come back. But I was too busy playing my own game to work out what was going to happen.'

Alan frowned, and scribbled in his notebook.

'What's that?' said Eoin. 'Do you have some idea about what happened?'

'No,' smiled Alan. 'It's just that France have scored,' as he pointed out on to the pitch.

Eoin lay back on the grass and stared at the grey clouds overhead. He decided that he needed to stop worrying about William and the trophy in case he got a headache, which he would have to admit to Neil. He was fed up with watching rugby though, and decided to give the rest of the game a miss.

He returned the bike to the Leinster Rugby offices and

rambled back to the accommodation block where the teams were staying.

'Howya Eoin,' came the call as he entered the dining hall. Charlie Bermingham was sitting with a group of boys including Paddy, Rory, Sam, Killian and Joe. 'How's your head?'

Eoin filled them in on his stay in hospital, and what the doctors had told him about missing the next game.

'Oh no, that's terrible,' said Sam, before quickly adding 'No offence, Joe.'

Joe smiled softly. 'No offence taken, Sam. In fact, I agree with you. Eoin's a much better out-half than me and I hope I can do as good a job as him.'

'You will of course,' said Eoin. 'No pressure now, but do you know that a good win over Italy should mean we reach the semis? Make sure that happens and we'll both be in the shout for the knock-out stages.'

'The Italian lads are a good laugh,' Paddy chipped in. 'I met a few of them who were in London in the summer and they're always up to mischief. I don't think they're here expecting to do anything except have some crack.'

After some more chat about the game Eoin stood up.

'I need a bit of sleep,' he admitted. 'Hospitals aren't great places to sleep. They keep waking you up to check are you all right.'

He wandered up to the dorm he shared with Paddy, James Brady and Jarlath Vasey, and lay on his bed.

He had just closed his eyes when he heard a cough. At the end of his bed stood William.

'Eoin, I do apologise for disturbing your sleep, but I have some news from the hunt for my trophy,' he started.

Eoin sat up. 'Tell me more,' he said.

'Well, remember how confused I was when I first met you. We know now that it was this trophy that brought me to this country, and the fact that I was drawn to visit you in your bedroom and elsewhere is clearly impor-tant – I believe you are the key to solving the whole mystery.'

CHAPTER 32

Eoin nodded slowly. What William had worked out made great sense – but what could *he* do? There were hundreds of policemen and women running around looking for the cup – if they couldn't find it, what hope had a kid?

'OK,' he replied. 'I'll keep my eyes open, but I'm not sure how I can help.'

'I'm *certain* you can,' replied William. 'But just don't keep your eyes open – keep your mind open too. There will be something in what you've seen and heard that will give you a clue.' His face darkened. 'We really must find this trophy – this is so important to me and to the whole sport of rugby. It's not just that it carries my family name, and that of my old school, but it repre-sents all that is good about being excellent at the sport. I've been learning about this "television" invention and I know that millions of people all over the world are looking at this tournament – and all they see is a stolen cup!'

Eoin promised William he would have another look

around and ask his team-mates had they seen anything during the match. He wouldn't be able to train for a few days so he would try to keep himself busy.

He was awakened two hours later by Paddy stomping into the dorm. He wasn't happy.

'You won't believe it, Eoin,' he growled, not bothering to apologise for waking him up.

'What?'

'We had a practice match at the end of training and Matthew went in a bit hard on Joe. He's only gone and cracked a rib.'

'Ah, no,' gasped Eoin. 'So he's out for Tuesday?'

'Yep,' replied Paddy. 'And Neil has already told me I'm playing out-half. I was really settled playing centre and now I have to switch and learn a load of new moves. And my kicking isn't as sharp as you or Joe.'

'Don't say that Paddy,' said Eoin. 'You're a brilliant out-half – sure that's where you were picked by Ulster in the summer and you got them to the final then. The moves aren't too complicated at all, and you'll have a great advantage playing alongside Sam.'

Paddy shrugged his shoulders.

'I don't know, Eoin. These games are huge – I'm finding it hard to sleep as it is and I'm not sure I'm even enjoying the whole experience. Is there no chance of you playing?'

'No, I'm afraid not. I didn't get a bad knock at all and they say there was no evidence of concussion but there's no way they're going to take that chance. I'm disappointed – but I have to agree with them.'

Paddy nodded.

'Now,' grinned Eoin, 'please go out there and make sure I have something to get back to when I'm allowed to!'

'Ach, sure I'll do my best but I'm not sure I'm up to it,' Paddy sighed.

'Stop that talk,' laughed Jarlath, who had just arrived at the doorway. 'Those Italy lads aren't much use, and sure you won't be on your own. The rest of us are pretty amazing anyway.'

Eoin laughed at Jarlath, who was always up for a laugh and a member of the Connacht team that had given Leinster such a lesson. That game in Limerick seemed like years ago, not weeks.

'Hey Jarl, what do you remember about the day the cup went missing?'

'Well, it's hard to remember anything, to be honest. We were getting such a pasting out on the field, and then you getting stretchered off was a bit of a distraction. I do remember seeing the cup just after you scored though, so it could only have disappeared after that. It's amazing they didn't find it though – everyone was searched leaving the ground. They even came into the dressing rooms to check our kit bags before we left.'

'Really?' asked Eoin. 'They must have been very thorough – how on earth did the thieves smuggle it out.'

'Or thief,' said Paddy. 'How do you know it was more than one?'

'Good point,' said Eoin. 'I'm very confused about that day, and it's not just because I got a bang on the head. I'm trying to work it out, but I think the ambulance driver took a longer route to the hospital, going over bumps and around bends when there was a straight clear run from the way he had come beside the pitch.'

'Ach, sure why don't you check it out on the computer?' suggested Paddy. 'One of those mapping sites will tell you in a second. Here, I have one on my phone.'

Paddy twiddled around with his smart-phone and discovered that the distance from the Belfield Bowl to the hospital was just 700 metres.

'But the ambulance ride took about ten minutes,' Eoin puzzled. 'They could have carried me down on foot in that time. Where on earth was he going?'

'Maybe he was new in the job,' offered Jarlath. 'He mightn't have known the area.'

'But the hospital is less than a kilometre away. He must have known the area,' said Paddy.

'Anyway, that's all very well,' said Eoin. 'But that's not going to help us find the trophy – or beat Italy. Do you want me to through the plans with you or not Paddy?'

CHAPTER 33

Paddy was a quick learner, and he, Sam and Neil worked hard on getting their tactics right for the game against Italy. There had been a bit of disrespectful talk among some of the players about the opposition, but Neil wasn't haven't anything to do with that. He hammered home his points about the Italians' strengths and made sure there was no complacency.

It worked, and Ireland ran out 38-3 winners with Paddy settling brilliantly into the role and kicking four of the six conversions as well as scoring a try. The result put Ireland in a stronger position, but as there was no chance of Italy beating the Kiwis, whether Ireland qualified or not now depended on the other results.

Alan kept Eoin updated on the situation with regular texts over the next few days, and also called over to watch some of the games. They arranged to meet in Belfield to watch the final two games of the pool stages.

'It doesn't matter who wins between Australia and England because they both have a smaller points difference than Ireland, so the loser will be below us anyway,'

Alan explained as they walked over to the ground. 'But the last game could be messy, because Scotland and South Africa both had big wins over France.'

'So what does that mean for us?' asked Eoin.

'Well, if South Africa win, Scotland can go through too if they stay within two points,' explained Alan. 'But if Scotland were to win, then the South Africans would just have to avoid defeat by more than fifteen points and we would be out.'

Eoin inhaled sharply. 'Oh dear, that's not great is it?' He liked the Scots lads he had met in London during the summer, but there was only one thing for it.

'Come on the Springboks!' he laughed. 'And of course the Aussies – for Charlie.'

The boys found a place to sit on the grassy banks opposite the main stand, and chatted. Eoin was embarrassed to admit that because of the lack of developments he had given up hunting for the William Webb Ellis Cup – and he wasn't looking forward to William's return.

'There's fewer policemen around today, too,' he observed. 'I suppose they're busy doing other things now the fuss has died down.'

'I suppose there's nothing left to protect here except the much smaller and less fancy trophy you're playing for,' Alan pointed to the group of four security guards who now stood beside the platform. 'That's a good example of closing the stadium door after the horse has bolted,' he chuckled.

Eoin laughed too, but then suddenly stopped in his tracks. 'What did you say about closing the stadium door?'

'After the horse has bolted?' replied Alan.

'No, forget the horse. Stadium door... bolted... lock... key...'

Eoin stared at Alan, and back at the security guards.

'I have it,' he says. 'I know how they got away with the trophy. But catching them and proving it is another story...'

'Hang on, Eoin, hang on,' gasped Alan as he trotted along behind his friend. 'Where are you going?'

'I'm going to talk to one of the World Rugby or IRFU guys. They'll know if there's any Gardaí around still working on the case.'

Eoin scanned the grandstand to see if he spotted anyone he knew. Right in the middle, carrying a clip-board, sat Neil.

'Eoin, are you here to watch the games?'

'Well, yes,' he replied, 'but that's not what I came to

ask you. Is there anyone around from the IRFU who might have anything to do with the missing trophy?'

Neil stared at Eoin. 'Trophy? Well, the union's security officer, Keith, is around somewhere. He's been very involved with the investigation.'

Neil stopped and looked towards the pitch where the teams were lining up.

'That's him there, the tall man with the moustache. Tell him…'

But Eoin never heard the rest of the sentence, as he took the steps two at a time in his rush to get onto the field.

He tapped the tall man on the arm.

'Sir,' he started. 'I was on the Ireland team on the day the cup was stolen. I think I know how they did it.'

CHAPTER 34

The IRFU official stared at Eoin, and checked his name on the card he had hanging around his neck.

'Eoin Madden. Well, Eoin, that's very interesting. Let me just finish up here and we'll have a chat.'

The official stood and watched as the game kicked off and checked his watch.

'Right, I can give you precisely four minutes. Come in here,' he added, directing Eoin to a prefab office.

'What's this about the trophy?'

'Well…' Eoin started, scrambling to put his thoughts in order. 'It started when Roger Savage was injured during the game, and was put in an ambulance. The driver must have been poisoned, as he was throwing up and had to abandon his ambulance just outside the back gate there.

'Then I was injured later and a *different* ambulance collected me. I only found that out later, but I was suspicious because he we went a longer roundabout way to the hospital.'

Keith looked baffled, and a little irritated.

'This means nothing, Eoin, you're wasting my time.'

'No, I'm not, honestly. There was a bit of delay getting going and I found out that the ambulance driver wanted to leave by the other gate because, he said, it was a much shorter journey through the college and out the main entrance. It was actually much longer and bumpier, and the gate was locked anyway.

'But he must have asked the security man guarding the trophies to get the key so he could have a chance to steal the trophy.

'The one thing I remember before we left was the driver dropping a kitbag on the floor of the ambulance and kicking it under the bed. The guys on the team said that the Gardaí searched all their kitbags, which put that idea into my head.'

The IRFU man nodded, and pursed his lips.

'How big was the bag? Did make a rattling noise?'

Eoin shook his head. 'I was lying down so I didn't have a great view, sorry.'

'But they had to leave you down at the hospital…' the IRFU man muttered. 'There might be CCTV pictures of the vehicle and the driver…'

He stood up quickly. 'OK, stay right here and I'll be back in one minute.'

He returned with the nice World Rugby official,

Fitzy, and three Gardaí, who looked excited. Eoin told them his story.

'That's not a bad theory at all,' said the senior garda. 'Have you any career plans yet? You'd make quite a decent detective.'

Eoin smiled. 'I had a bit of spare time after I got injured so I spent a lot of time thinking about the case.'

'Well if you decide, give me a call,' she smiled, handing him her card.

The detectives quizzed Eoin for almost an hour, asking him to go over his story several times while stopping him to ask questions every few seconds.

When they were finished they thanked him and told him they would be in touch, and Eoin left the office buzzing.

He found Alan and told him what happened, filling him in on his theory about the theft of the William Webb Ellis Cup.

Alan had loads of questions, and was delighted to hear that it was his mention of locking the stadium door that had led to Eoin coming up with his solution. He was completely captivated by the story, but he was rudely interrupted by a cheer from the grandstand alongside.

Alan looked up to see boys in blue shirts celebrating a try. He checked the scoreboard and, with a look of horror, returned to his calculations.

'What's up?' asked Eoin.

'We're in trouble,' he replied. 'If the Scots convert this they'll be one point ahead of us on points difference. And there's less than two minutes left.'

CHAPTER 35

The conversion sailed over and Eoin winced. It pained him to remember back to his try against the All Blacks and how he would definitely have put the conversion over had he not been flat on his back.

'Oh no!' groaned Alan. 'We're a goner. What are the chances of South Africa getting up the other end?'

Eoin shrugged. The Baby Boks were already in the semi-finals; he didn't expect them to make any great effort to score again.

As the time ticked away, the Scots started to relax and sense the place was theirs. But a Garryowen from their scrum-half failed to make touch just outside the Spring-bok 22 and it was collected on the bounce by the South African winger. He looked up to see the Scots trotting after the ball and spotted a gap. Like the African ante-lope that sprang across their national crest, the winger hit top speed almost immediately and burst through the fingertips of the defence. With one delicate change of direction he was away, charging 70 metres at full tilt towards the posts.

The score brought the crowd to its feet, both for the brilliance of the move and what it did to the result, which ensured the host nation would qualify for the last four.

The Scots boys' heads fell, and one or two burst into tears. The South Africans were delighted, and whooped their joy as the final kick went over the bar. But none of these displays of emotion were as extraordinary as that shown by Alan, who took his Ireland replica shirt off, twirled it around his head and went off on a trot along the top of the grassy bank, strutting like a chicken and singing 'We Are the Champions'.

Eoin was amused by his pal's display, if a little embarrassed that he thought singing about being champions was the right thing to do when Ireland had just about scraped into the last four. Still, it was well worth celebrating. 'Put your jersey back on, you'll get pneumonia,' he laughed. 'Or some chicken disease anyway.'

Alan leapt in the air and embraced Eoin. 'Wasn't that try fantastic? And we're into the semis!'

'It's brilliant,' agreed Eoin. 'I wonder who we're playing next.'

'Australia,' blurted Alan. 'Sorry, I thought you knew.'

'No, but that's not too bad. I was afraid we'd have to play New Zealand again.'

'They organise it so the best second-placed team can't play the team from the same group. I had all the different options worked out before the game,' he said, showing Eoin a piece of paper that looked like a drawing of a plate of blue spaghetti.

Eoin took one look at the calculations and handed the paper back.

'I'll take your word for it,' he chuckled.

The boys spotted Neil in the stand and raced over to him.

'Well coach, you've got to be happy with that,' smiled Eoin.

'Yes, that was fantastic. I feel sorry for the Scots, but it would have been very hard on us to be knocked out that way. Now we have to get you match-fit as soon as we can – we're playing the Wallabies just three days from now. Their coach is over there, I must go over and have a word.'

Neil pointed over to the corner of the stand where a man in a bright gold blazer was deep in conversation with someone they knew well... Charlie Johnston.

As Neil greeted the Australia coach, Charlie looked across to where the boys were standing. He grinned sheepishly, and shrugged his shoulders.

The next three days passed in a whirl for Eoin. His sitting-out period was over and he was able to take a full part in training. He slotted back in perfectly at No.10, and Paddy was happy to move back out to centre. Joe Kelly was distraught that his tournament was over but Neil asked him to stay with the squad and enjoy – as a non-combatant – whatever lay ahead.

After their last training session was finished Eoin sat down beside Joe and asked him how the Irish side looked from the sideline.

'You've a great eye for a move, when to run and when to kick,' he told him. 'You must have some ideas for what we need to do against the Aussies.'

'Thanks, Eoin,' Joe smiled. 'I have noticed a few things you do differently to me, but they've been successful for you so don't go changing at this stage.'

'Every day's a school day, Joe. My grandad's always saying that. I'm always open to suggestions.'

The pair chatted away and compared their different approaches. Joe made a good point about Sam.

'When he picks up the ball after a ruck or a scrum he always has a look where the backs are before he gets the pass away. If he had his look while the ball was still inside the set-piece he'd have that extra second to make the pass. I was only in the team for one game so I didn't want to mention it, but you seem to know him pretty well.'

Eoin nodded. Sam *had* been slow against Castlerock in the warm-up game, but then he had been much better against the All Blacks. He said he'd have a chat with Paddy first to see if Sam would mind this being pointed out.

One good thing about Joe's injury was that Neil had to rejig the squad a bit, and as he was well covered at out-half with Paddy and Eoin, he decided to bring in some cover on the wings, which meant a call-up for the delighted Dylan.

After dinner that night Eoin went for a run with his friend and when they reached the rugby ground they paused to lean against the gate.

'Look out there, look at that field,' said Dylan. 'That's where it's all going to happen over the next few days – you're going to become a national hero with five million people knowing your name, or you're going to disappear back into being an anonymous nobody who's adored by only about five hundred kids. That would be a big win, wouldn't it?'

Eoin had been thinking of the game the next day,

but hadn't quite thought of it in that way. And he was more distracted by a familiar figure who was wandering around in front of the grandstand on the far side of the pitch.

'Who's that?' asked Dylan. 'He's a weird looking character. Is he in fancy dress?'

Eoin laughed.

'That's your man you were talking to back in Castlerock, isn't it? The lad who invented rugby!' asked Dylan.

'Yeah, that's him,' replied Eoin. He's going mad looking for the trophy because it's named after him. I hope the Gardaí are able to find it.'

'He's waving now. Do you want to go over to him, he seems like he wants a chat?'

'Time to go, I think,' said Eoin. 'We're under a curfew tonight so let's get back to the living quarters before we get into trouble,' he said, before turning and jogging away from the sports ground.

Chapter 36

If Eoin thought he had escaped William he was sorely mistaken. As he brushed his teeth later that night he noticed a stern-looking face over his shoulder in the mirror.

'Are you avoiding me, young sir?' asked the ghost.

'Oh… hi, Will,' muttered Eoin. 'Well, not really. It's just that as far as I know they still haven't found the trophy. I had an idea that it had been stolen by the ambulance man, but the Gardaí haven't been able to track him down. They found him on CCTV driving into the hospital but they lost him after that.'

'CCTV? What's that? … Oh, never mind. Please let me know if you hear anything at all.'

Eoin nodded, and said he would, before William disappeared.

Later, as he lay his head down on his pillow, he remembered what Joe had said about Sam and resolved to say something to him over breakfast.

There was a much bigger crowd next day, with television cameras all around the ground as both semi-finals would be played back-to-back. The press box was packed too, and Eoin had been a bit embarrassed earlier when he was shown the newspaper previews, which all insisted that his return was a great boost to Ireland.

He grinned across at Charlie Johnston as the teams lined up for the anthems but he was a bit taken aback when his old friend turned his head and looked down at the ground.

Eoin put the slight out of his mind and began his pre-match concentration ritual, slowly tidying everything away in his brain except the game plan. He took one look over at the tournament trophy before setting that – and the hunt for 'Bill' – aside, too.

Australia were a tough side and, if truth were told, a little dirty. Neil had pointed this out to Eoin the day before and they decided that they could punish this and score a lot of points by taking penalties when they were in range. Eoin had practised kicking for ninety minutes after training and was happy he could slot the ball over from almost angle.

The Wallababies started with a bang, conceding a penalty in the first minute – duly kicked by Eoin – and then tackling Sam off the ball, which cost them the services of their open-side flanker for ten minutes.

Eoin noticed that Sam's passes seemed to come to him even slower than usual after that, and he kicked himself for not talking to him that morning. After one pass that was delayed needlessly – and saw them both floored – he decided not to waste a moment.

'Listen, Sam, I don't know if you even know you're doing it, but every time you get the ball out of the scrum you stop and look back to see where I am. If you did that before you take it out you'd have some extra time. That could be crucial.'

Sam looked a little bit put out, but he nodded and said he'd try it next time.

The quality of the ball coming back to Eoin improved after that, but he noticed that the Aussie forwards were still quicker on to him than he had ever experienced before and seemed to know when he was going to pass, kick or run.

Eoin grew more and more frustrated, as Ireland attacks were snuffed out as soon as they had begun. Luckily the Aussies were not able to mount much of their own, and their regular fouling meant Ireland were 6-0 up at half-time.

'They keep closing me down, coach,' seethed Eoin as Neil gathered the team around in a huddle. 'It's like they know what I'm going to do.'

'Maybe they do,' said Paddy. 'Sure isn't their Number Eight your old mate from Castlerock and Leinster. He knows all your moves and when you're going to make them.'

Eoin realised with horror that Paddy was right. That's what Charlie had been talking to his coach about in the grandstand, and that's why he had been so embarrassed in the pre-match. He was letting the Aussies know all he had learned about Ireland's key player over the years they had played together.

'That's a bummer,' said Neil. 'But look, don't panic. You've a good footballing brain. Change your moves and the way you set yourself up to pass or kick – it will confuse them. Maybe try something a bit funky now and again like a crossfield kick or a missed pass.'

Eoin smiled, reassured by Neil's ideas and deter-mined to put it right.

He grinned at Charlie Johnston again as they lined up for the second half, and tapped the side of his nose as if to say 'I know what you're up to'. Charlie grinned back and shrugged his shoulders.

CHAPTER 37

The Australians came back hard at Ireland and scored a try very early in the second half. Eoin tapped over yet another penalty to keep Ireland 9-7 ahead as the game approached the hour mark.

Neil made several changes, including bringing on Rory for Sam, but told Eoin he wanted him there till the end. Having only played one game he wasn't as tired as the other guys, and the coach believed his ability to kick the ball from any angle was going to be crucial.

Eoin extended the Ireland lead to 12-7 with a few minutes left, but a blunder by Rory let the Aussies away and their winger scored a diving try in the corner. They watched nervously as the Australian out-half lined up the conversion and were mightily relieved when he put it five metres wide.

'Phew,' said Rory. 'Sorry I messed up there. We still have a chance in extra-time.'

But as the final whistle blew the referee gathered all the players around him.

'Right young men that was a most entertaining game.

You may not know this, but this tournament is being played under some experimental regulations that may be used in the Rugby World Cup next year. And one of those is to abolish extra time and go straight to a goal-kicking competition.'

Eoin gulped. Paddy's face fell. Rory opened his mouth wide – 'But... do we have five goal-kickers?' he asked.

'That's nothing to worry about,' grinned the referee. 'This new-style contest is actually for just one player on each side.'

Now it was Eoin's turn to open his mouth. 'Oh no, you're joking?'

But the ref insisted that he wasn't and explained the rules of the shoot-out. The ball would be placed on five different points spaced out evenly along the 22 metre line, ranging from one touchline to the other.

'That's just like your training sessions down in Ormondstown Gaels,' said Dylan, who had joined the group on the field along with Neil and the rest of the staff.

A cameraman came onto the field and pointed his camera at Eoin, who realised that he now had millions of people around the world staring at him and waiting for him – and his Australian counterpart – to decide the game.

When the referee had settled everyone down and the touch-judges were standing at the posts, the contest began.

Eoin had won the toss and decided to go first, reckoning a successful kick would heap even more pressure on the man following.

Far out on the left, he smacked the hall hard and high and it fell in an arc just inside the near post. The Aussie looked rattled, but managed to follow him successfully. Their next three kicks were successful too, and the tension in the crowd was at its highest as Eoin stepped forward to take the final kick.

As a right footer, he always found those kicks the hardest as he liked to curl the ball in slightly. But that was much trickier to do from that angle with the much smaller target than in a straight-head kick.

He took his steps back and sideways, steadying himself and checking again that there was no wind. He looked at the posts and began his run.

'Whummmp,' he hit the ball perfectly square, and waited for it to do its part of the job. It sailed towards the righthand post before it took a tiny curl inside – the result was signalled by a huge roar from the packed stadium and the cheers from his team-mates behind him.

Eoin walked back to join them, on the way passing

his Australian opposite number whose face looked grey. Eoin took a deep breath and waited for the kick. He scanned the crowd, and was delighted to spot Dixie had turned up with Eoin's parents. There too, standing on the grassy bank, were William Webb Ellis and Brian Hanrahan.

The Australian was extremely nervous, probably remembering that he had taken a conversion from that very spot just twenty minutes before and had fluffed it. He did his best, but the weight on his mind added weight to his legs and he just couldn't get distance on the ball, which trickled under the posts.

The crowd erupted, and Eoin was again swamped by his team-mates in green. A TV reporter came dashing out to ask him questions, and Eoin gave him some embarrassingly stupid answers about 'game plans' and 'leaving nothing out on the park'.

When things had calmed down – and Eoin had sought out Charlie to say 'hard luck,' and swop banter about being a traitor – the teams had left the field so that New Zealand could play South Africa in the second semi-final, Eoin joined his family in the grandstand.

He filled them in on all the excitement he had been through since he last saw them in the hospital and how he had come up with his theory about the ambulance and the trophy.

Dixie's face suddenly turned pink.

'Oh, dear,' he said. 'Perhaps I should have spoken up earlier. When your parents were in visiting you in hospital I stayed outside in the car – there in the multi-storey carpark. I was just watching the world go by when the big white ambulance you came in drove past me at great speed. I thought that was a little odd – I thought the ambulances would park somewhere else – but then it pulled in beside the exit doorway and the driver got out. He collected a bag from out of the back and disappeared down the stairs.

'I thought it was a little weird, but…'

Eoin never heard the rest of the sentence as he was already half way down the steps in search of Fitzy and Keith.

CHAPTER 38

Eoin found the World Rugby man standing at the trophy stand chatting to another official, and explained to him what his grandad had seen.

Fitzy asked him to come with him to the prefab out the back where he had been days before. The Gardaí arrived and Eoin went over the story again before they asked him to bring them to Dixie.

His grandfather was a bit shocked when the detective tapped him on the shoulder to ask could they have a word with him, but Eoin reassured him and the old man seemed to enjoy being sucked into the drama.

'This is like Sherlock Holmes,' he whispered to Eoin at one stage. 'I'll have to bring along my pipe next time to help them solve it.'

Once he had told the police the full story, and they had checked it over, the senior Garda told the Maddens that they could go. Eoin led Dixie back to the grand-stand.

'Well that was quite a turn up,' laughed his mum.

'I wonder who they'll get to play me in the movie

– *The Webb Ellis Trophy Mystery* they'll probably call it,' chuckled Dixie.

'Well, it won't be George Clooney,' teased his mum. 'Maybe his father?'

Eoin said goodbye to his family, who had a long drive ahead of them and would be returning to Dublin in a few days for the final. The out-half hero rejoined his team-mates, who were watching the closing stages of the second semi-final.

He had discussed who he would prefer to win with Alan a couple of nights before, and they settled on South Africa. But having won the semi-final, Eoin realised that narrow defeat to the All Blacks still really rankled and he desperately wanted to make amends.

'Come on the Kiwis,' he called, as the team in black battled to defend their four-point lead.

His team-mates stared at him. 'Are you mad in the head?' asked Ollie.

'No,' Eoin replied. 'It's just that even if we win the final against South Africa, that defeat to New Zealand will hang over us and they'll always say we weren't the best team in the competition. I want to play the Kiwis – and beat them.'

The rest of the boys stopped, and nodded. As one, they took up the chant 'All Blacks, All Blacks' drawing surprised stares from supporters nearby who had earlier heard them rooting for the Springboks.

And five minutes later they let out a huge cheer as the final whistle blew and they knew that New Zealand would be their opponents in the tournament decider.

'Right lads, tonight is your night to blow off a bit of steam. We'll take you out later for a bit of bowling and a burger, so back you head to get cleaned up and changed and we'll see you down at the hall in ninety minutes.'

Eoin rambled back with Paddy and Sam, all the way buzzing at their great achievement.

'Did anyone see me on the telly?' asked Eoin. 'I hadn't a clue what to say. I hope I didn't make a fool of myself.'

'I'm sure you were fine,' laughed Sam. 'But I bet you'll have a load more of that to do before the final – there were dozens of journalists there today.'

Eoin groaned. 'Oh no, I hate talking about myself and I don't know enough about rugby – I'll come across as a total spoofer.'

'Just tell them that the campaign to win the World Cup was all Neil's idea and he worked so hard to come up with the plan,' said Paddy. 'That'll get you plenty of brownie points and show you're modest and don't want any glory for yourself.'

Eoin laughed, but agreed with Paddy too. Rugby was

a team game and anyone who thought they were the only reason why the team won would soon be found out. Eoin was good at kicking a ball, and working out when to pass or run, and a few other skills, but he would be totally useless in the front row of the scrum, or trying to win a line-out. It was important to point out all the other great players he was lucky enough to share a shirt with.

CHAPTER 39

It was just after midnight when William came to visit. Eoin had been asleep, but was awoken by a cold breath across his cheek.

'I'm sorry, young sir,' whispered the ghost, urgently. 'But you must come, and at great haste. I have found the scoundrels who stole the trophy.'

'What… where…' Eoin shook his head to try to dismiss his sleepiness. He stared at William and saw the panic in his eyes. He dressed quickly, checked he had his mobile phone, and threw on a hoodie.

'Follow me,' whispered William as they sneaked past the room-mates who were all snoring away, oblivious to the mysterious visitor.

The ghost led him out of the building and down past the sports ground and out to the six-lane highway which ran past the university.

As they walked along the footpath lit by streetlights Eoin shivered, although he wasn't cold. William explained that he had been wandering aimlessly for days around the district, when one night he had felt a strong force summoning him down to this place where he was sure the trophy now lay.

'It's down here, not too far,' he said, 'perhaps half-a-league.'

Eoin was confused. 'A league?'

'Ah, of course, I keep forgetting you are more than two hundred years younger than me. A league was what we once called three miles – so you can work out what half-a-league is?'

Eoin laughed. 'That's not too bad. I'm sure you've found our world a lot harder to work out.'

'I have surely,' said William. 'Between television and CCTV and those miniature trains that people drive along the roads…'

'Miniature trains? Oh you mean cars!' Eoin laughed.

He felt his pocket to check his phone and he saw the power was down to two per cent. He groaned as it flickered and died. He hoped he wouldn't need it later.

They covered the ground quickly and arrived at a dark laneway just outside the sleeping village of Donnybrook. Eoin was a bit nervous looking down it, and the screech of a cat didn't make it less spooky. But one of the flickering streetlamps suddenly burst brighter and he was at least able to see where he was going.

'They went in there,' whispered William, pointing at a

garage door that was battered and rusty, but from which was hanging a shiny, brand new padlock.

Eoin tiptoed up to the side and noticed that light was escaping from several cracks and holes in the metal door. He peered through the largest one he could find.

Inside he spotted three men sitting around a table, in the middle of which was perched the William Webb Ellis Cup. He strained to hear what they were saying.

'But no one will buy it,' said one man, 'It was a stupid thing to steal, it's too recognisable. It's all over the papers and the telly.'

'Hang on there, it was *your* idea,' said another man. 'You were with me when we saw it out in the college when we were delivering furniture that morning. You even came up with the plan!'

'Yeah, and who nearly killed that ambulance man with too much of those crushed-up tablets?'

'There's too much going on with the guards – I can't get anyone to touch it…' said the first man.

'There's only one thing for it then,' said the second man, 'It must weigh about ten pounds – we can melt it down and sell it as silver scrap. We'd get about two thousand from a lad I know who deals in the stuff under the counter.'

Eoin's eyes and mouth opened wide in horror, and he

gasped at what he had heard.

'What's that noise?' asked the third man, who Eoin recognised as the fake ambulance driver.

'I dunno,' said another. 'Did you hear something?'

'I thought I did,' he replied. 'It must have been a cat. Let's finish up here and get ourselves home. I'll check with my mate to see what he'd offer for it as scrap. We'll meet here this time tomorrow – can you bring the gear to melt it down, Christy?'

Eoin didn't wait around to see the men leave, haring around the nearest corner in case they wanted to investigate further the noise he had stupidly made.

'What do you think of that?' asked William.

'It's terrible!' replied Eoin. 'And we need to contact the police as soon as possible.' He looked again at his dead phone and shook his head.

They decided that William would wait at the criminals' den in case they came back and moved the trophy, and Eoin would contact the Gardaí first thing next morning.

Eoin was really rattled as he wandered through the suburbs in the dead of night, wondering how he would explain what he knew to the police. His only companions as he walked were cats and foxes and they could give him no advice as he made his way back to the campus.

CHAPTER 40

Sleep wasn't easy either, as Eoin kept seeing the three thieves in his head, and hearing them make their dreadful plan.

He woke early and decided to jog down to the Belfield Bowl to see if there were any officials or Gardaí around. He was surprised to find it locked up, with just one security man in a hut at the gate.

'Ah, there's no more rugby here,' he told Eoin. 'There was so many people looking for tickets for the final tomorrow that they've switched it down to the Leinster stadium in the RDS. It'll be nice and quiet here now.'

Eoin thanked him, and wandered off, wondering what to do. He had training in less than an hour, and needed to fuel up at breakfast. As he considered how long it would take to run down to the nearest Garda station, another ghostly visitor whispered to him from the bushes.

'Hello, Eoin,' said Brian. 'I hear you're in the middle of another adventure. But you need to be very careful now, from what William tells me those lads look like trouble.'

Eoin nodded, and explained that he was going to tell the Gardaí, but would have to wait till after training.

'Do you not have a telephone number for the police lady?' Brian asked.

'I do, of course,' replied Eoin, puzzled. 'But I didn't notice you there that day?'

'Ah, I get to lots of places you don't see,' laughed Brian. 'I'm trying to keep you safe you know!'

Eoin fished the card from his pocket and dialled the number. The detective didn't answer so he left her a message to call him, and trotted back to the lodgings for breakfast.

Training was excellent, with Neil giving his analysis of the Baby Blacks' strengths and weaknesses and how Ireland could overcome the disadvantage of having less physical power. Eoin knew he had to play a huge game and wanted to begin concentrating on that to the exclusion of everything else – but the stupid trophy kept cropping up in his mind.

They watched a video of the first game after lunch and discussed how they could improve. As soon as that was over Eoin sneaked around the back of the dressing rooms to make a phone call. The senior Garda, Detective Garda Sweeney, answered and Eoin told her what he had seen.

'So you're telling me you were wandering around the backstreets of Dublin at one o'clock in the morning and just "came across" these people? What are you not telling me here?'

Eoin was lucky that the Garda wasn't there in person or she would have seen him blush.

'I couldn't sleep so I went out for a jog. I spotted the ambulance driver and, well, I followed him,' he lied. He hated telling fibs, especially to the police, but if he told her the truth he would probably be locked up himself and miss the World Cup final.

'All right, stay where you are and I'll come over to collect you and you can show me this garage.'

Eoin returned to the changing rooms and dressed quickly, telling Neil that he was wanted by the Guards and would be missing for a while.

'OK,' said Neil. 'But not too long I hope. We have a huge game tomorrow and your curfew is ten o'clock. We have a team meeting, too, at seven pm, and I expect you to be there.'

Eoin nodded and hurried away to await the arrival of the policewoman.

When Garda Sweeney arrived, she talked to him for twenty minutes, weighing up his story and clearly finding it hard to believe parts of it. But in the end she seemed to take his word for the important part of the tale and asked him to show her the crooks' lair.

As they drove down to the area she filled him in on what the police had discovered.

'Your grandfather's tip was very useful,' she told him. 'We found the ambulance and the fingerprints we got off it are of a man who is very well known to us. He's not staying at his usual address however and our officers are searching for him everywhere. So it's excellent that we know where he will be tonight.'

Eoin had a good sense of direction and even in daylight was able to pick out the landmarks he had spotted the previous night, and guided the Garda close to the garage.

The detective parked her car at the corner and asked Eoin to walk down the alley, and to stop and tie his shoelaces outside the door of the garage.

Eoin did as she asked, checking while he did so that the padlock was firmly on the door.

'Good man, Eoin,' she said on his return. 'You never know whether places like this are being watched. We'll get a plainclothes team down to scout out the area and find who owns the garages on either side.'

She drove him back to the Garda station. 'Can you

not bring me back to Belfield?' asked Eoin. 'I have a meeting soon and a big match tomorrow and I have to get back to that.'

'I'm sorry, Eoin,' she replied. 'You've been caught up in what will be a major Garda operation. We will need to go over your statement again and again. And for security reasons we won't be able to let you go back until the operation is over. We will call your parents and they will be allowed to come here, but nobody else – unless they'd like to nominate a teacher to come in and sit with you instead.'

Eoin gulped. What would Neil say? He asked the Garda could he phone the coach but she said she couldn't allow that while the operation was ongoing.

'But the coach will go mad,' he said. 'We've the final tomorrow and I have to be at the meeting…'

'I'm sorry, Eoin,' she replied. 'Perhaps I could send him a text message, but we can't allow you to contact anyone who was involved in the rugby that day – they could be witnesses or involved in the case.'

Eoin's head fell. This was a disaster. He should have kept his nose out of the whole mystery. He turned to face the wall and fought back the big tear that was trying to break out and run down his cheek.

CHAPTER 41

The hours dragged, and there was little to do in the Garda station except watch news channels on TV and read the newspapers. Some of them had articles on the Under 16 World Cup and he was delighted to see his own name cropping up every time Ireland was mentioned.

'Teak-tough number ten' was how one reporter described him. 'Midfield dynamo', wrote another. Was that a compliment? He made a mental note to check those terms out in his dictionary when he got home.

The guards brought him sandwiches, and later a burger and chips, but after one bite Eoin remembered he was still expecting to play in the World Cup final in a few hours, and that chips probably weren't the best fuel for him, so he ate the burger, but not the chips.

A teacher arrived from Castlerock with a message that his parents would see him tomorrow, but Eoin told him he would be OK on his own and the teacher returned to the waiting room to mark a pile of Christmas exam papers.

It was after midnight when Detective Garda Sweeney returned with a dark fleece for him to wear. 'It could get cold out there,' she told him. 'We'll need you to sit in the back of a Garda car and identify the men as they go in. Zip up and let's go.'

Eoin followed her outside and sat in the car while the rest of the unit assembled.

'The rest of the plainclothes team are down there already,' she told them. 'Our job is to identify the men, hopefully catch them in the act, secure their arrest, and return this trophy to its rightful owners.'

Down at the alley, Eoin sat in the plain, unmarked car parked fifty metres away, checking both entrances using the wing mirror. About 12.50am he noticed a man walking towards him who kept checking over his shoulder that he wasn't being followed. Outside the garage he stopped again, checked both ways, but didn't see anything amiss and opened the lock to let himself in.

'That's one of them,' said Eoin.

Soon after the second man arrived, and right on one o'clock the ambulance driver sneaked silently along the street and slid sideways under the shutter.

'That's them all,' Eoin confirmed, and Garda Sweeney

relayed the message via her walkie-talkie.

Nothing happened for a minute or so, but Eoin tried hard to remain calm when William just floated out through the metal door. He was waving wildly at Eoin and pointing at the sparks which were starting to fly out through the cracks in the garage door. Eoin pointed the sparks out to the detective who immediately called out 'Go!'

What happened next was a blur to Eoin. From all parts of the street emerged Gardaí wearing blue jackets. Garda Sweeney banged on the shutter and immediately a group of four guards carrying guns lifted the shutter and raced in.

Eoin braced himself to hear shots, but none came, and after a very long minute the trio were led out one-by-one, handcuffed behind their backs and heads bowed. A Garda van sped around the corner and the men were lifted into it while the armed guards stood watch.

As soon as they had been taken away the detective returned to the car where Eoin had watched all the action unfold.

'OK young hero,' she grinned. 'The good news is the men have been detained and the mission has been a success. But it was a close one. They had the blow torch fired up and were just about to melt the handle off the trophy. Do you want to see it?'

Eoin nodded.

'Well I'm afraid it's a crime scene now so I can't admit you, and you can't touch it before the fingerprint team has finished either. But come over here and take a look.'

He followed her down to the garage he had spied on the night before and peered into the darkness. The garda torches lit up the corners as the detectives went about their work, but Detective Sweeney shone hers onto the table. There, no worse for its adventures, sparkled the William Webb Ellis Cup.

CHAPTER 42

The teacher drove Eoin back to the accommodation block just after two o'clock in the morning, but he found it very difficult to sleep. His mind raced as he went over the dramatic raid and he shivered when he replayed seeing the sparks and the damage the blowtorch could have done to the beautiful trophy.

He eventually dozed off, but woke again at six-thirty. He stared at the ceiling and thought about the day ahead. The first game against New Zealand had been a bruising affair, but the Irish boys had really come together as a team and Neil had worked out some good plans.

About seven o'clock he heard the other boys stirring so decided to get up and get an early breakfast. As he dressed, Paddy sat up in bed, stretched and yawned.

'Eoin, it's great to see you. What time did you get in at?'

Eoin told him, and briefly explained the night's events.

'I'm going down for an early breakfast,' he added. 'Didn't get much food last night and I want to see Neil.'

'Oh,' said Paddy. 'Have you not seen Neil yet?' He

bowed his head.

'Why?' asked Eoin. 'What's up?'

'Oh nothing,' replied Paddy, blushing. 'Neil said he wants to see you first thing though.'

Eoin made straight for the breakfast room and found Neil eating at a table with the other coaches.

'Ah, Eoin,' said Neil. 'Can I have a word?'

Eoin followed the coach out into the corridor.

'I'm afraid I won't be using you in the starting fifteen today,' began the coach.

'But…' started Eoin, before Neil raised his hand. Eoin stared at the floor.

'We made strict curfew rules for this competition and we can't change them now just because it's the final, and just because it's you.'

'But the guards wouldn't let me leave,' said Eoin.

'Look,' he went on, 'I don't know what you got your-self caught up in, but we needed you at the team meeting and when you didn't show we had to change our plans. You were a key member of the team and we just couldn't go ahead without you. I have picked Paddy at out-half and we'll have you on the bench in case there are changes needed. Again, I'm sorry to have to do this but if I allowed one rule to be broken then respect for all the others would go.'

'OK,' replied Eoin, looking Neil in the eye. 'I see your point. Thanks.'

He went back inside and collected his breakfast, and as he sat down Paddy arrived.

'Oh, Eoin, I'm so sorry. Neil told us not to tell you until he talked to you first.'

'It's OK, Paddy, seriously. Don't worry about it.'

Eoin didn't enjoy his first proper meal for twenty-four hours as he was constantly interrupted by boys commiserating with him. Others had heard the reports of the cup's discovery on the news and wanted Eoin to give them the inside story.

'Is there a reward?' asked Dylan.

Eoin laughed. 'I never asked,' he confessed. 'But I'm not surprised you wanted to know.'

'Well, don't forget all the help me and Alan gave you. That cup must be worth millions.'

Eoin chuckled, and laughed again as he heard Dylan telling the lads at the next table that he would be getting a half-a-million euro reward.

The boys were ferried down by coach to the RDS Stadium two hours before kick-off. To warm-up they had a few stretches and a run-around on Leinster's home pitch in front of the empty stands before going back inside to change.

Eoin sat quietly, not getting involved in the chats with Sam and the centres like he usually would. He felt a bit of an outsider, and was angry that he had missed out on such a big game. He didn't think Neil was being fair, but clung to the coach's promise that he would get a run if necessary.

As kick-off neared Neil spoke, keeping his message simple and doing his best to calm the boys' nerves. Because he was off the team, Eoin wasn't nervous at all, which made him feel a bit strange.

He patted Paddy on the shoulder as they left the dressing room – even in the circumstances he was delighted that it was his friend who was getting a chance to shine, and told him so.

'Och, I don't know Eoin,' replied Paddy. 'There's a few lads there looking at me funny. They know I'm not as good as you.'

Eoin joined in the kick-about on the pitch, and waved at his family as they took their place in the stands. As the players were running through their drills the loud-speaker crackled into life and the match announcer welcomed the supporters to the Royal Dublin Society grounds.

Here are the teams for day's game, he announced, reading through the New Zealanders first. Then he came to the Irish team:

'Backs… Matthew Peak, Kuba Nowak, Sam Farrelly, David Bourke, Ollie McGrath, Paddy O'Hare and Sam Rainey. Forwards… James Brady, Ultan Nolan, John Young, Jarlath Vasey, George Savage, Oisín Deegan, Charlie Bermingham and Noah Steenson.'

Eoin looked up to where his family were sitting and shrugged his shoulders. Even from that distance he could see they were surprised, maybe even shocked. With a heavy heart he turned, put on his tracksuit top, and took his place on the bench.

CHAPTER 43

Just as in the Pool game, Ireland were quickly made aware of the power and strength of their opponents, but this time the referee was ready and flashed his yellow card for the first serious offence. The penalty gave Paddy a chance to get points on the board. With the ball inside the 22 and straight back from the left-hand post, it couldn't have been easier for him, but he hooked the kick and the ball flew harmlessly wide.

Eoin bit his lip and ignored the mutters from Rory and Dylan on the bench, with whom Neil's selection had not gone down well.

'Shut it, Dylan,' he whispered. 'Let's get behind the lads.'

But the grumbling grew louder as it became obvious that Paddy was having a nightmare. He hurried his kicks and failed to find touch, and whenever he decided to run he hesitated and was buried by black-clad tacklers.

Eoin felt desperately sorry – Paddy didn't want to be there and would prefer to have been playing in the centre. But if Ireland's out-half wasn't on top form then the game would be over before it got going.

Just before half-time Paddy tried to get the ball out to his centres, but a slow pass allowed a speedy Kiwi to charge through the middle and dispossess David. In the blink of an eye he was running under the posts and finally getting the scoreboard moving.

The two-point conversion went over just as the half-time whistle blew and Neil, with a serious expression, raced ahead of his team into the dressing room.

When Eoin got there the coach was in deep conversation with the rest of his staff, pointing to his iPad and making urgent hand gestures. He allowed the team to get their drinks and sit down before he spoke.

'I'm delighted with much of what we did out there – the way you battled and kept your discipline,' he said. 'It was a pity they scored before half-time because you deserved to be on level terms at the very least. But I think the main problem was at my end in the selection of the team and I'm going to make a change to redress that balance. I'm going to bring Eoin on at out-half, and slot Paddy in at inside centre.'

There was silence among the team, although a few of the boys nodded. Paddy grinned across at Eoin, who offered a thin smile in return. He was glad Paddy wasn't being blamed for the setbacks and would still get a chance to play.

The announcer was informing the crowd of the changes as the teams ran back out on to the pitch and Eoin was pleased to hear a large cheer when his arrival was revealed.

'OK, Sam, let's get this show on the road,' he grinned.

The New Zealanders gave him a warm welcome, a late tackle leaving him flat on his back. One of their props leaned over him and grinned in his face.

'You back for more punishment? Watch out for the next one.'

Eoin said nothing, deciding he would concentrate on remembering that prop's face so he could wave his winners' medal in it at the end.

CHAPTER 44

E oin got his chance to start showing the Kiwis that they had crossed the wrong player when Ireland were awarded a penalty kick on the ten-metre line. There was a strong wind gusting down the ground, but he found his range instantly and brought the score to 7-3.

The Baby Blacks obviously expected to be miles ahead by that stage and grew impatient that Ireland's defence was holding firm. Eoin floored the right winger with a crunching tackle as he tried to break on the outside and the Kiwi took exception to it. He stood up quickly and swung a punch at Eoin's head, but the Irishman was expecting it and ducked, and the blow landed square on the nose of the prop who had been sledging him earlier.

'You've broken it, you drongo!' he roared, clutching his face as the blood started to flow.

Eoin fought hard to keep his face showing concern, but broke into a grin when Sam winked at him.

'What are you laughing at?' roared the prop, by now covered in blood.

The All Black medic arrived and told the player he would have to leave the field, and the referee issued the same instruction to the winger.

'I don't care that you missed your opponent,' he told him. 'There's no room for that thuggery in the game.'

The Kiwis were stunned, in one moment of madness they had been reduced to fourteen men and also needed to replace one of their best players. Eoin beckoned the Ireland team to huddle around him.

'OK, we can win this now. They are going to be in disarray for a few minutes so let's hit them hard and get the ball out to that wing where they won't have cover.'

The new prop wasn't as big, or fierce, as the original selection and James drove hard at the next scrum, and won the penalty. It was outside goal-kicking range, but Eoin had other plans. He signalled he would kick to touch down the right wing but at the last second switched direction and speared the ball towards the opposite corner. The move had been fruitful for him earlier in the competition and this time it worked a treat. Kuba came racing up the wing, collected the ball and sprinted for the line. He was held up just short but turned and fed the ball back to Sam Farrelly who was following up well and the centre crashed over for a try.

The cheers could have been heard out in Castlerock,

Eoin reckoned, and he was still on a high when he slotted over the conversion to give Ireland a three-point lead.

There was more than ten minutes left for Ireland to defend the advantage, and it turned out to be the longest ten minutes of their young lives. They tackled and chased, heaved and fought and never allowed the Kiwis to even get near their twenty-two.

'Keep your discipline, keep your shape!' roared Charlie, and his team never let him down. The final whistle came and Eoin sank to his knees, before he was submerged seconds later under a sea of muddy green shirts.

Just as the aftermath of the Pool defeat to New Zealand was a blur to Eoin, so was the next few minutes – but in a much nicer way. Everywhere he turned there was a smiling face and someone who wanted to hug him or thank him. He made his way over to the New Zealanders and shook each of their hands, even that of the prop whose nose was now swollen enormously.

'Sorry you got the biff, mate,' he told him.

'Yeah, me too,' came the reply, 'but fair dues, you really showed us how to battle. Well done.'

Eoin grinned and turned to face the grandstand. He spotted his parents and Dixie, who was accompanied by Mr Finn, and returned their wave. He also noticed something strange about the platform where the two trophies now stood. Besides the six security guards who stood watch, there were two other men hovering nearby. One wore a black, red and yellow hooped shirt, the other the clothes a man might have worn two-hundred years before.

Brian and William lifted their arms in salute, wide grins lighting up their long-dead faces. William pointed to the trophy that bore his name and mouthed 'Thank you'. Eoin gave them a thumbs up and turned to rejoin his delighted friends.

TURN THE PAGE TO SEE MORE GREAT BOOKS ABOUT EOIN MADDEN AND HIS FRIENDS

RUGBY SPIRIT

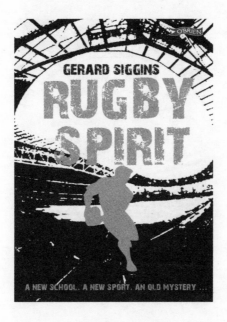

A new school, a new sport, an old mystery...

Eoin's has just started a new school ... and a new sport. Everyone at school is mad about rugby, but Eoin hasn't even held a rugby ball before! And why does everybody seem to know more about his own grandad than he does?

RUGBY WARRIOR

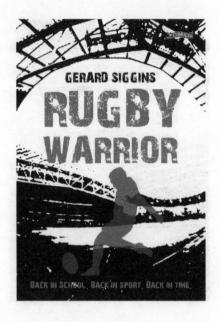

Back in school. Back in sport. Back in time.

Eoin Madden is now captain of the Under 14s team and has to deal with friction between his friend Rory and new boy Dylan as they battle for a place as scrum-half. Fast-paced action, mysterious spirits and feuding friends – it's a season to remember!

RUGBY REBEL

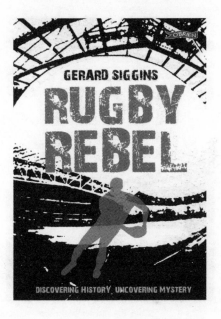

Discovering History - Uncovering Mystery

Eoin Madden's been moved up to train with the Junior Cup team, which is hard work, plus there's trouble in school as mobile phones start going missing!

But there are ghostly goings-on in Castlerock – what's the link between Eoin's history lessons and the new spirit he's spotted wearing a Belvedere rugby jersey?

RUGBY FLYER

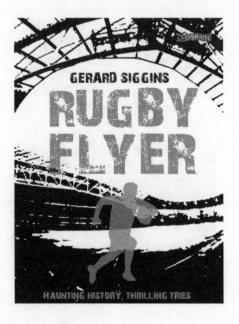

Haunting history, thrilling tries

Eoin and his new friends are taken on a trip to Twickenham to play & watch rugby. There, he meets a ghost: Prince Obolensky, a Russian who played rugby for England, scored a world famous try against New Zealand in Twickenham and later joined the RAF and died in WW2.

obrien.ie